The Snake River Bounty

As a young man, Ben Hollinger hunted down and killed the outlaw gang who murdered his family. He now lives a very different life as the marshal of a sleepy cattle town.

But his hopes for a peaceful future are shattered when he kills a young troublemaker who has forced him into a gun fight. The boy's father, Nate Thornton, owns the biggest ranch in the territory and he puts a bounty on Hollinger's head.

Violence sweeps the town as every local gun-hand tries to hunt Hollinger down to claim Thornton's ransom. His only hope for survival is an alliance with the rancher's daughter, Cordelia, but will she really be prepared to side with the man who killed her brother?

The Snake River Bounty

Bill Shields

A Black Horse Western

ROBERT HALE · LONDON

ISBN 978-0-7090-9121-9

Robert Hale Limited
Clerkenwell House
Clerkenwell Green
London EC1R 0HT

www.halebooks.com

Typeset by
Derek Doyle & Associates, Shaw Heath
Printed and bound in Great Britain by
CPI Antony Rowe, Chippenham and Eastbourne

CHAPTER ONE

THE FIRST KILLING

Billy Thornton was trouble. He had been since he was a boy. Ben Hollinger watched him ride in at the head of the Tumbling T wagons and felt a twist of tension in his gut. He was a problem the town of Bannack could do without.

'Last Friday of the month, just shy of noon,' Bracken observed, looking at his pocket watch. 'Thornton folk is nothing if not punctual.'

Miles Bracken, Bannack's elderly doctor, was seated outside the town marshal's office with his left foot resting on the hitching rail. He saw the troubled look on the marshal's face and nodded his agreement.

5

'I know what you're thinking, Ben. Them boys is pure trouble.'

'Not all of them, Doc,' Hollinger said.

'Well no, not all of them. Mostly just Billy and his friends. His sister used to be, but not any more.' He shot a wry grin at the marshal. 'Cordelia's grown up some this last year, as I'm sure you've noticed. Getting more like her mother than old Nate. She'd be right passable if someone just got her to wear a dress now and then.'

Hollinger didn't rise to the bait. The entire town knew about Cordelia Thornton's endless teasing of the marshal. Teasing was all it was, Hollinger told himself; there could never be anything more between them.

The three wagons pulled up in front of Orchin's General Store. Cordelia Thornton climbed down off the lead wagon. Hollinger allowed himself a lazy smile as he took in the usual absence of feminine dress. Cordelia was dressed the same as the cowhands she led into the store to help her with the supplies, she just filled the clothes better. A wide-brimmed hat was pulled down low over curling, honey-blonde hair that was cut back to above shoulder length.

'Yes sir,' Bracken said. 'Someone needs to take that girl in hand.'

Hollinger turned his attention to the two outrid-

6

ers who now galloped on past the store, following Billy Thornton down to the Remuda saloon, Tom Carrow and Jinks Screeby. They were two of Billy Thornton's closest followers, and two more evil-tempered hardcases you'd be hard-pressed to find. They clung to Billy's shirt-tails because he was Nate Thornton's son, and they figured he could get away with just about anything. In the past, he pretty much had.

Hollinger had heard rumours of trouble in other towns along the Snake River, but Nate Thornton had always bought off or scared off anyone who came complaining about his son. Thornton himself had little respect for any law but his own. Since being appointed town marshal a year ago, Hollinger hadn't seen much of the man who owned the largest cattle spread in the territory, but he'd heard tell that Nate Thornton was a mean, cruel man who had been getting worse since the death of his much younger wife a few years back.

His son, Billy, had been smart enough not to cause too much of a ruckus in Bannack, so far. There had been some drunken brawls and general bad behaviour, twice leading to a night in the cells, but nothing too serious. Hollinger figured that Billy had been warned about making trouble too close to home.

Bracken took his foot down off the hitching rail,

pushed up off the chair and stretched. 'Well, I reckon I better pay me a visit out to the McHenry place. Martha's about due any time now. John's about as jumpy as a cat on hot coals. You'd think it was the first time his wife had given birth, not the sixth.' He followed the marshal's gaze down towards the saloon. 'Hope they don't give you too much trouble this time.'

Hollinger shook his head. 'Billy's too afraid of his pappy.'

'I don't know, Ben. When that boy gets to drinking all thought of his pappy's displeasure gets lost somewhere in the whiskey bottle. Anyways, I'll be seeing you come evening.'

After Bracken had departed the marshal did a turn around the town. Bannack wasn't that large, just an average-size cattle town. The main thoroughfare, Bradley Street, was the wedge-shaped business centre of the town, with a general store, drug and cigar store, two saloons, a hotel, a barber, a dentist and a bank. Miles Bracken had his practice up above the general store owned by Frank and Jenny Orchin, next to a lawyer's office. The Presbyterian church and the town hall bookended the street.

Running parallel to the main thoroughfare, Conover Street had an express office, a blacksmith, stables and a furniture emporium that doubled as an undertaker's parlour. A maze of smaller streets forked off these two like spokes in a wheel.

Hollinger took a turn through the alleyway between the stables and the vast bulk of the furniture emporium and on to Drover Street, down towards the stockyards on the far side of town. Except for the usual commotion around the stockyards the day was peaceful. The sun was still high and the day was hot, but Hollinger could feel the slight chill when he walked in shadow. The Indian summer the town had enjoyed for the last few weeks was almost over, and at night the autumn winds were bringing a change. The old-timers were saying that all the signs pointed to a bad winter ahead.

Back up on the main street he was just passing the general store when a bulky sack of flour hit him in the chest. Behind it there was a wide-brimmed hat with honey-blonde curls escaping from under it.

'Sorry about that. Can't see where I'm going.' Cordelia Thornton stuck her head round the side of the flour sack. 'Oh! It's you, marshal!'

Cordelia's face lit up with pleasure as she looked at the tall marshal. She liked what she saw. She always had. Ben Hollinger was lean and rangy, with broad shoulders and big hands that looked like they could bend iron. He had a long, narrow face with a square, determined-looking chin and pale-blue eyes the colour of winter ice. Under the black Stetson he had a thicket of unruly black hair. Standing there in his black leather vest and dark-blue shirt he gave a comforting impression of dependability and physical strength.

As a lawman those were fine qualities to possess, but Cordelia had heard tales of a different Ben Hollinger, of a more desperate and damaged man who had done questionable things in the past. Those stories sharpened her interest in him even more.

'Hello Cordelia,' Hollinger said, tipping his hat politely.

'Ben, you know I hate being called that. It's Cord, not Cordelia. Cordelia makes me sound like some society rose, and I ain't that, or hadn't you noticed?'

Hollinger grinned. 'Doc Bracken was just saying as how fine you'd look in a nice dress, with your hair allowed to grow out and put up all fancy like.'

Cord snorted. 'Was he now? I guess you'd like that as well. Some sweet-smelling, swooning little flower you could treat like a silly child. Men don't want a woman who might best them in a fair fight.'

'Well, I don't reckon on fighting you, Cord, even if you did assault a peace officer with a flour sack. You know you could get thirty days for that?'

Cord snorted out a short laugh. 'You fixing to carry me off to your jail, marshal? I warn you, I bite and scratch like the worst she-cat you ever imagined.' She heaved the flour sack on to the nearest wagon. Behind her three more of the Tumbling T ranch hands came out, heavily burdened with provisions.

'I don't doubt it,' Hollinger said.

'You could find out for sure. Real easy.'

Hands planted on her hips, Cord was now giving him a look that held both promise and challenge. It was a look that made Hollinger uncomfortable. He averted his gaze to the wagons, before his own eyes betrayed him. He found Cord Thornton irresistible, even in that unfeminine get-up, but allowing her to see that would be a mistake he had no intention of making.

'Those wagons are getting well filled,' he said. 'Looks like you're expecting some kind of siege. You could hold out for months on what you got there already.'

Cord shrugged. 'It's a big ranch, marshal, and everybody's saying it's going to be a long hard winter.'

Hollinger shaded his eyes, looking up at the bright sunshine and blue skies. 'Winter's still a ways off.'

'You know my father. He likes to be ready for anything.' An amused gleam sparkled in her eyes. 'Do I make you nervous, Ben? I mean, every time I'm around you get jumpy as a scalded polecat. It don't look good for a big tough lawman to be afraid of a little girl like me. Townsfolk might get to thinking you're soft on me.'

'Cord. . . .' For a moment Hollinger was lost for words. 'You are not a little girl. Not any more. And yeah, you make me jumpy.'

'What's the matter, Ben? You think you're too old for me? Why, there's only eight years between us. My father had nearly thirty years on my mother.'

It was one of the few times Hollinger had heard Cord refer to her mother. Lisa Thornton had died when Cord was fourteen years old. Nobody ever spoke about how she died, but Hollinger had heard rumours about the woman's unhappiness. Nate Thornton couldn't have been an easy man to live with.

Eight years, Hollinger thought. But I guess it's what you do in those years that ages you. He said, 'You're right, Cord, I do think I'm too old for you. And I'm pretty darned sure that your pappy wouldn't approve of you talking this way.'

Cord laughed. 'You think I worry much about what my—'

At that moment young Jed Lowry, who worked in the saloon, came running down the street. 'Marshal! Marshal! You gotta come right now! We got trouble!' He pointed back towards the Remuda.

'Hold on, Jed! What's wrong boy?' Even as he asked the question, Hollinger knew what was wrong. Billy Thornton was in the saloon, so it was an easy guess.

'He's gonna kill Leto! He's holdin' a gun on him and he's madder than hell!'

Leto Picken was one of Hollinger's two deputies. The other one, Jake Fallon, was over in Clearwater, delivering a prisoner to the marshal there. Leto tended to be hot-headed, and he had a personal grudge against Billy Thornton.

Cord started to follow as Hollinger headed towards the Remuda, with Jed Lowry at his heels. 'No, Cord! You stay here!' He didn't want her anywhere near her brother. The two of them were usually at each other's throats, and Cord could easily provoke her brother to some greater folly.

There was a tense silence as Hollinger entered the saloon. Most people were clustered near the batwing doors, ready for a fast exit once the shooting started. The Remuda was a long, low-ceilinged room, with a bar running most of the way down the left side. Thick wooden supports and stout beams held up the roof, and for a moment the marshal couldn't see Billy Thornton.

Leto Picken was standing with his arms at his side, gun still holstered, with Tom Carrow and Jinks Screeby either side of him. Neither one had a gun out, but their stance indicated a readiness to violence. Leila Wendell, the owner of the Remuda, was standing well back, holding one of her girls, a fiery redhead called Sally Devon, by the arms. Sally had her hands held up to her tear-stained face.

Hollinger could guess what had happened. For a while now his deputy and Billy Thornton had been rivals for Sally's affections. It had come to blows a few weeks before, and had ended with Billy spending the rest of the night in a jail cell, and Leto getting a stern talking to from the marshal. Hollinger had known that wouldn't be the end of it.

Hollinger looked into the long mirror that ran behind the bar and saw Billy. He was behind one of the pillars, facing down the deputy. Moving through shafts of bright sunlight from the shuttered windows, the marshal came around the wooden support from the side opposite his deputy's position. Leto was clearly angry, his face stained red with helpless fury, but he was frightened too. Hollinger could see why. Billy Thornton was holding a gun, a Colt Frontier double-action, with its long barrel pointed at the deputy, and he was working himself up to using it.

'You think I give a good goddamn about that badge?' he snarled. 'I told you to keep your hands off my girl. You should have listened. The marshal ain't here to save you this time.'

'Billy! No! Don't do it!' Sally screamed. She was trying to pull away from her employer, but Leila had a tight grip on her. 'I ain't your girl. You leave Leto alone.'

Hollinger spoke quietly from behind Billy. 'Do

what the lady says, Billy.' Thornton froze at the sound of his voice. Carrow and Screeby saw him for the first time as he stepped out from behind the pillar. They both had their guns holstered. Billy was the only threat. 'Just drop that gun and step away. Nobody has to get hurt here.'

'He ain't got his gun out, Billy,' Screeby said, eyeing the marshal's still holstered sidearm. Hollinger saw Billy tense, clearly thinking about it.

'You really think you can turn and shoot before I put you down.' Hollinger's voice was calm and reasonable. 'You try it and it'll be the last mistake you ever make.'

'You ain't putting me in your jail again, Hollinger. I been there twice, there ain't gonna be no third time. This sonofabitch ain't going to stand there laughing at me again.'

'Jail is just where you're going, jackass,' Leto snarled.

'Shut up, Leto!' Hollinger snapped. 'That's no way to handle the situation. You should know that.' Hollinger guessed that Billy was as much afraid of losing face in front of Sally as he was of facing down the marshal. He turned to Leila and said, 'Take her out of here.'

As Leila hustled the protesting girl away, Billy said, 'Big man! Ordering folks around! Big law-dog boss man! I never can figure what my sister sees in you.

You ain't telling me what to do, not any more. And you ain't locking me up, not this time.'

Hollinger said, 'I'm not locking you up, Billy. Just drop your gun and you can ride on out of town. Do it, son, before this gets any worse. And you, Leto, you head on out of here.'

Billy hesitated, then said, 'OK, marshal. You get that sonofabitch out of here and I'll leave peaceably, 'cause if he stands there one minute more I swear I'm gonna plug him.'

'All right, Leto. You head on out, and you get well clear of this saloon. Get going.'

For a moment Hollinger thought the situation was under control, but then Leto, as he made to walk away, gave Billy a sneering look that sent Billy's temper flaring. As he pulled back on the trigger of his Colt, Hollinger pulled his own gun and clubbed him across the back of the head. The shot went wide of Leto and hit the opposite wall.

Billy dropped to the floor and Hollinger snatched the pistol out of his hand. Carrow and Screeby dropped their hands to their gunbelts, but stopped short when Hollinger brought his Colt single-action army revolver up to cover them.

'OK, that's it, boys. You can help Billy up, and then you're all coming over to the jailhouse with me.' He looked at his deputy. 'Leto, I told you you to get out of here.'

'I can help you get them over to the—'

'Leto! You heard me! You get the hell out of here. Cord's down by the general store. You tell her to let her pappy know I have Billy in a cell again.'

At that moment he sensed movement behind him. Cord wasn't down at the store. She was standing right behind him. As he turned towards her, he said, 'Cord, I'll have to take Billy—'

Before he could finish Cord's mouth opened wide in a panicked yell. 'Billy! Don't!'

Hollinger swung back towards her brother. As Screeby helped him to his feet, Billy reached down and pulled Screeby's navy revolver from where it was stuck in his belt. Flame leaped from the barrel and Hollinger felt shards of wood explode from the pillar beside him, hitting the right side of his face.

The marshal reacted with lightning speed. He hammered back the Colt and fired, saw blood erupt like a flowering red blossom on Billy's chest. The boy dropped like an empty sack. Hollinger knew that he was dead. There hadn't been time for anything else.

He swung his Colt on Tom Carrow, the only one of the three still armed and standing. Carrow threw his arms high, eyes wide with fright.

'Billy!' He heard a broken voice behind him and turned. Cord Thornton was staring at her dead brother, a look of absolute horror twisting her ashen face. Then she turned her gaze on the marshal.

17

'You killed him,' she said accusingly. 'You murdered my brother.'

CHAPTER TWO

TEN THOUSAND DOLLAR BOUNTY

'I guess I got all of it,' Bracken said, holding up a bloodied shard of wood. 'You're damn lucky none of it hit your eye.'

On entering the marshal's office an hour before, he'd placed a lamp on the desk and told Hollinger to tilt his head back. He'd worked methodically, removing the wood chips that Billy Thornton's slug had blasted from the support into the right side of Hollinger's face.

'Thanks, Doc.' Hollinger started to push himself up from the chair.

'Hold on,' Bracken said. 'You're not going anywhere yet. You need a dressing on that mess. None of it was too deep, but you don't want it infected.'

'I haven't the time,' Hollinger said, standing up. 'I have to get out to the Tumbling T. I can't imagine how Nate Thornton's going to deal with this.'

'You can't?' Bracken looked surprised. 'Well, I can. You go out to that ranch and he'll likely have you shot on sight. If he don't do it himself there's enough wild young bucks working for him who'll see the job done.'

'Doc's right,' Leila Wendell agreed. She was an impressively large woman, big-busted, with wide hips and a mass of upswept hair the colour of autumn leaves. She had a no-nonsense reputation with the cowhands who frequented the Remuda saloon, but those who knew her recognized the warmth and humour in her soft hazel eyes. No one had ever pinned down her exact age, but somewhere north of fifty was reckoned to be close enough.

Besides Bracken and Leila there were two others present in the marshal's office. Frank Orchin had appeared right after the Tumbling T hands had thundered out of town, and Leto Picken paced around the room, clearly agitated and with his head down. Hearing Bracken's remark, and Leila's agreement, his head snapped up. 'Anybody tries any gunplay they'll join Billy in the cemetery. I'll see to that,' he said.

Leila shot him a pained look. 'Hell, Leto, ain't you caused enough trouble for one day?'

'Me! It was Billy Thornton what started it!'

'You should have walked away, son. You're supposed to be a peace officer. That means you keep the peace, not get into fights over saloon girls. Especially not fights that lead to a killing.'

'Sally ain't just no saloon girl, and I weren't about to let her get pawed by trash like Billy Thornton.'

Hollinger looked at his deputy, saw the high colour in his face and the defiance in his eyes. He saw the guilt as well. Leto knew the kind of trouble he'd likely brought down on the marshal. Guilt and anger, and the need to prove himself more than just a callow young fool: those could be a dangerous mix. There was going to be trouble, and the marshal knew he had to get Leto out of harm's way or the boy was likely going to get himself killed, and maybe not just himself.

'Leto,' he said, 'in the morning you're going to head over to Clearwater, and you're going to stay there until I say you can come back.'

'What?' Leto was outraged. 'Hell, no! You need me here, and I ain't afraid of—'

Hollinger raised a palm to stop him. 'But I am afraid. I'm afraid of you making the situation worse just by being here. You do what I say. You get yourself over to Clearwater, and you tell Jake what's happened here. Tell him to get back here as soon as he's done with delivering his prisoner.'

'Should have been back by now,' Bracken said. 'Got himself a sweetheart over there, I reckon.'

Leto wasn't happy, but Hollinger let him stomp about, muttering to himself.

'It's a pity Sam Mooney didn't ride in with them,' Frank Orchin said.

Sam Mooney was the foreman out at the Tumbling T, and a good man. Any time he accompanied the wagons into town trouble never got started. He kept a firm check on his people, and especially on Billy and his friends.

Hollinger asked about Billy Thornton's corpse. 'Has Edgar moved him down to his parlour yet.' Edgar Wheelock was the town undertaker, as well as being its only furniture salesman.

'No,' Bracken told him. 'Cordelia insisted on loading him into one of the wagons. She took him home. Says he'll be buried on Thornton land.' Bracken paused, chewing at his moustache the way he did when he was worrying over something. 'I never seen that girl in such a state. Her brother and her never was close, but she never seen him shot dead before. She was crazy mad. I thought for a moment she was going to get a gun and come after you herself, Ben.'

'I killed her brother.' Hollinger's voice was bleak.

Leto wasn't the only one filled with guilt and regret. 'Right in front of her. I could have tried to stop him without killing him.'

Leila stepped over to him, put a hand on his shoulder. 'You stop that right now. You didn't have no time for anything fancy. If you'd hesitated even a second more he'd have killed you, Ben. Maybe Cord as well. She was standing right in back of you and he was shooting wild, not caring who got hit. She was bleeding when I saw her last, so them woodchips hit her as well. That's how close she was to taking a bullet.'

Hollinger knew that she was right, but he couldn't begin to think what Cord and her father were feeling right at that moment.

The man who stood in Nate Thornton's study was a picture of weary defeat. His shoulders were slumped as though forced to bear some great weight.

'So, Svenson, you're finally ready to sell to me?' Thornton asked.

In his time Nate Thornton had been a great bear of a man, tall and straight and heavily muscled, with a direct gaze that had unsettled many an enemy. But he was over sixty now, and the hard life he'd once led and the whiskey he'd consumed had taken its toll. His eyes were little holes of bloodshot mean-ness, and his large frame was sagging visibly. He eased up out of his chair with some effort.

'I got no choice,' Svenson said, his tone accusing. 'My cattle are run off, my well poisoned. I can't get no one to work for me.'

Thornton fixed him with a look of bloodshot astonishment. 'You make it sound like I got something to do with that.'

Svenson shifted nervously. 'No. Not at all, Mr Thornton. I wasn't saying that.'

'I should hope not, seeing as how I got my lawyer standing right there.'

A rotund, balding man called Hamilton Bell stood opposite his client, his posture one of eager readiness. He nodded to Thornton, then spoke to Svenson. 'I have the papers right here, Mr Svenson. If you'll just sign we can give you a draft for the money.'

As his lawyer relieved Svenson of his land – land that Thornton had wanted for some time – the rancher went through to the cavernous room that was the centrepiece of the house. Bookshelves lined one wall, filled with books that Thornton had never read, while expensive ornaments and paintings adorned the others. The chandelier over a massive dining table was an elaborate crystal creation, and the floor was covered with an ivory-white carpet of softened sheepskin that Thornton was particularly pleased with. It was an Axminster, the carpet of choice for wealthy English country homes. This was the family room, although the family that it had been created for had been cut short by his wife's death.

Thornton scowled as he thought of his dead wife. He'd wanted a large family, a dynasty to carry on his name, and she had cheated him out of it. Left him with a crazy daughter who dressed so that no man would ever want her, and who seemed to lean towards worthless no-accounts like his own ranch hands and that annoying marshal his son had told him about. His son was his only hope, but he had no illusions about him. Billy's abilities didn't seem to reach much beyond drink and trouble, but maybe with a few more years on him, and the proper marriage that he himself would arrange. . . .

Thinking on his son's shortcomings didn't do much for Thornton's peace of mind. He poured himself a large whiskey and went over to the window. On a rise beyond the ranch buildings he could see the black iron of the sideways leaning T. Beneath it, a convoy of wagons was kicking up a lot of dust.

'Why are they coming in so fast?' he asked himself.

To kick up that amount of trail dust the supply wagons had to be travelling at speed, and not be overburdened with the supplies they had gone into town to collect. When he saw that his daughter was driving like some demon out of hell, with Tom Carrow and Jinks Screeby galloping alongside her, he felt something cold slice deep into his gut.

'Billy!' he whispered, figuring it could be nothing else.

He had always known his son had a way of making trouble for himself. He'd pulled him out of enough scrapes for it not to have escaped his notice. But, hell, he'd been a wild one himself in his youth, wild and reckless as boys tend to be while they're learning to be men, but he'd turned that wildness into ruthless enterprise, built up the biggest ranch in the territory, and finally tamed that reckless nature. He'd figured that Billy would do the same. If a few people got hurt along the way, that was their lookout. You took care of yourself and your own.

Now he sat in his high-backed chair before a spluttering fire that was dying in the hearth. He was oblivious to the creeping chill in the high-ceilinged room. Billy was laid out in an upstairs room. The same one in which his dead wife had been laid out, after she'd been pulled out of the Snake. He raised his head and looked at the people gathered around him. Cordelia was sitting on the sofa, her hands twisting together like things in agony. Sam Mooney, his ranch foreman, was standing, hat in hand, his face grim. Hamilton Bell stood close beside him. Tom Carrow and Jinks Screeby had just finished telling their version of events at the Remuda saloon. They looked frightened as Nate Thornton fixed them with a hard stare.

'That's the way it was, Mr Thornton,' Screeby finished. He was a skinny, ragged-looking man with dark stubble and nervous eyes in a thin, undernourished face. 'That marshal, he never gave poor Billy a chance. Billy weren't even armed. He just shot him down. I tried to give him my gun, but it weren't no use. Then him and that deputy turned their guns on Tom and me. We couldn't do nothing, or we'd have been gunned down as well.'

Tom Carrow, a more handsome man than his scarecrow-like friend, still had a shifty-eyed look that warned most people to be wary of him. He said, 'That's the truth, Mr Thornton. That marshal's a killer for sure. Murdered Billy in cold blood.'

Sam Mooney was watching Cord, who had been shifting uneasily all through Carrow and Screeby's testimony. There were scratches on her face that she hadn't explained.

'That the way it was, Miss Cordelia?' he asked. He knew Ben Hollinger, and doubted any word that came from the mouths of Billy's two good-for-nothing friends. They'd never been any good as ranch hands, being more interested in helping Billy to get into trouble. The only reason he'd kept them on was because Billy was the boss's son and he'd insisted.

'Well, Cordelia?' her father snapped, glowering at her from under lowered brows. 'You got anything to add?'

Cord's eyes were still glistening with tears, but she'd had time to think about what happened, to see it over and over again in her mind. The pain of her brother's death was stabbing at her heart, and her anger was still directed towards Ben Hollinger, but what she was hearing from the two ranch hands was giving her some discomfort.

She shook her head, slowly and almost unwillingly. 'That's not right,' she said quietly. 'Billy grabbed for Jinks's gun. He started shooting before the marshal did. He might have hit me as well.' She touched the scratches on her face.

Her father scowled. 'Pah! I know you got yourself set on that sonofabitch marshal. Billy never got done telling me how you was drooling over him every time you clapped eyes on him. Now you're planning to defend the man who murdered your brother?'

'It isn't like that.'

'The hell it ain't! You get out of my sight, and you stay out of my sight until you get your thinking straight.'

Cord stared at him for a moment, her red-rimmed eyes overflowing with fresh tears, then she fled from the room.

After she'd gone, Nate Thornton fell silent for a

time. The other men in the room shifted about, not sure if they should speak or just leave. When Thornton eventually lifted his eyes to them, they were blazing with barely controlled fury. He said, 'Hamilton, my guess is we can't do nothing legal, is that right?'

The lawyer shook his head. 'Of those present at the killing I'd say that most of them would side with the marshal. They're all his friends and supporters. They'll testify that your son fired first, and that what the marshal did was legal.'

Thornton considered for a moment, before coming to a decision that both surprised and horrified Mooney and Bell. 'All right, a bounty then. That should get it done. Ten thousand dollars!'

Carrow and Screeby exchanged interested looks.

'Pardon me?' the lawyer said, thinking he hadn't heard right.

'Ten thousand dollars on that marshal's head. I want you to put out the word.'

Hamilton Bell stared at his client, his face aghast. 'Nate, as your lawyer I have to warn you against this. You can't put a bounty on a peace officer. Do you know the trouble you're going to bring down on yourself?'

Sam Mooney looked shaken. 'Boss, you can't do this.'

'The hell I can't!' Thornton snarled. 'I want

justice! I want that sonofabitch dead! There's ten thousand dollars for anyone who kills Ben Hollinger.'

Carrow and Screeby headed into the stables, hoping to settle down in one of the empty stalls, out of sight of Sam Mooney. They knew for sure that, with Billy dead, the foreman was going to get rid of them as fast as he could.

'What do you reckon?' Carrow asked, once they were hidden from view.

'I think that bounty the boss is offering is right tempting,' Screeby said, a greedy gleam in his eye.

Carrow nodded his agreement. 'He ain't too happy with us, that's for damn sure. He thinks we should have got ourselves shot along with Billy. I don't reckon on getting shot.' He gave Screeby a cautious look. 'If we try for that bounty, we gotta do it real careful like. I heard some stories about that marshal, about some killing he done before he came to Bannack.'

Screeby answered with a sly grin. 'Don't you worry none. The way I plan on doing it, he won't even see us coming.'

CHAPTER THREE

WORK FOR THE UNDERTAKER

The following morning Hollinger led his big dapple-grey out of the stables on Conover Street. The town was already busy as he walked him over towards his office. He saw Miles Bracken waiting on the board-walk outside the barbershop. He knew he was in for a talk on the wisdom of riding out alone to the Tumbling T, but his mind was set on it. He owed it to Nate Thornton, and to Cord. Besides, he was the law in Bannack. He couldn't hide in town after killing the rancher's son, and he had no intention of riding out there at the head of a bunch of armed men.

'I guess it won't do no good telling you you're

31

being a damn fool.' The doctor started his argument as the marshal tethered his mount to the hitching rail and stepped up on to the boardwalk.

'I got no choice, Doc.'

'At least take a few men with you.'

'How would that look?' Hollinger asked. 'Riding in with an armed posse to express my regret over shooting dead Nate Thornton's son, and to explain what happened.'

Across the street Leto Picken came out of the marshal's office, packed and ready to ride. His horse was hitched to the rail. He looked sullenly over at them, not at all happy with being sent out of town.

'That boy don't look too grateful about you keeping him safe,' Bracken said.

Hollinger moved aside to allow a young mother to pass with her brood of three children, twin boys and a baby she cradled in her arms.

Bracken doffed his hat. 'Morning, Sasha. How's little Joseph's cough?'

As Sasha paused to answer the doctor there was an agitated movement behind her. Hollinger recognized a face in the crowd. Tom Carrow, his gun drawn, was pushing clear of the people around him. As he started shooting, Hollinger yelled a warning and stepped backwards off the boardwalk, falling into the mud of Bradley Street as the hot wind of a bullet parted the air next to his head. Someone was screaming.

As he pulled his Colt, he heard Leto yelling, 'Marshal! Look out! It's Screeby!'

More shots followed the warning yell, but they didn't come from Carrow's gun. Hollinger hammered two slugs towards Carrow, as the crowd around the gunman cleared. Carrow was punched backwards by the bullets. He fell to his knees, then tried to pull himself up again.

Gunfire sounded from the far side of the street. Hollinger turned his head and saw Leto firing, then the deputy collapsed across the hitching rail, clutching at his gut. His head jerked as another bullet hit him in the neck, throwing a ribbon of blood into the air. People were running in all directions, trying to get clear of the gunfight.

The marshal rolled backwards, coming up into a crouch as he aimed his Colt at a white-faced Jinks Screeby. Before he could shoot, one of the twins ran headlong into the street. In a panic, Screeby grabbed the boy and backed off towards the corner of the barbershop. Hollinger got to his feet, keeping his gun aimed at the skinny frame cowering behind the kicking child, until he heard Bracken yelling behind him.

'Ben! He's not down yet!'

As Screeby bolted for the corner, shoving the boy towards Hollinger, the marshal swung around in time to see Carrow staggering to his feet and raising his gun arm. Hollinger fired three more rounds, each one hitting Carrow with a dull slapping sound. He staggered, then fell backwards, crashing through the barbershop window. Hollinger saw the horrified look on the barber's face, a second before he started off after Jinks Screeby, chambering rounds into the Colt as he ran.

As he rounded the corner he heard the pounding of hoofs, and saw Screeby riding out of the stables on Conover, his skinny body bent low over his mount. He was down the alleyway between the stables and the furniture shop before the marshal could take aim. There were still too many people about who hadn't found cover yet. Hollinger couldn't chance a shot at the retreating rider. He holstered the gun and went back to where Leto had slid off the hitching rail and was now lying in a widening pool of dark blood.

Bracken knelt over him. Spurting blood from the neck wound darkened his shirt front. He told Jed Lowry to go and fetch his bag, but the look he gave Hollinger said it was no use. Leto was coughing blood, pain and terror clear in his face as he stared up at the marshal with rapidly dulling eyes.

People were gradually filling the street again, crowding around the shattered barbershop window and a body that lay close to it, and around the hitching rail under which the dying Leto lay. There was shock and horror on every face.

Bracken turned an ashen face on the marshal. 'Sasha Barlow's dead. Carrow got her with that first wild shooting.'

Hollinger looked back to where Leila Wendel and Jenny Orchin were hurrying the twins and the baby away from their mother's body.

'I think the baby's all right,' Bracken said, 'but I got to check on him.' He looked down at the deputy. 'He's not got too long, Ben.'

'I'll stay with him,' Hollinger said. He was dimly aware of Leila's barman, Dan Backus, trying to clear the crowds off the street. Frank Orchin was helping. Hollinger heard him saying softly, 'Come on, folks, allow the poor boy to die without an audience.' Sally Devon pushed past him, tears blinding her as she slumped down beside Leto and clutched at his hand.

The marshal, along with an almost hysterical Sally, stayed by Leto's side until the light died from his eyes. When at last he looked up Hollinger saw Edgar Wheelock coming down the street towards them. He had a bad feeling that the undertaker was going to have more work before this was over.

Jinks Screeby was shaking as he stood before Nate Thornton. Thornton was staring at him with something between distaste and hatred.

'We tried, Mr Thornton, me and Tom. We tried to

kill Hollinger. I got that deputy though.' He grinned through blackened teeth, eager to please. 'I got him good, I know I did, hit him twice at least. That ought to be worth somethin'. I mean, it was him that got Billy all riled up and got him killed.'

'And where's Carrow?' Sam Mooney asked. The foreman was scowling at him like he was something unpleasant he'd discovered stuck to his boot-heel.

'I think the marshal might have killed him,' Screeby admitted.

'But you didn't wait to see for sure, huh? You just skinned on out of there, saved your own hide.'

'Like the way you didn't back my son,' Thornton added.

'Now wait a minute, boss.' Screeby sounded aggrieved, and frightened too at Thornton's tone. This wasn't the reaction he'd expected. 'We didn't have no chance in the saloon. Hollinger had a gun on us and—'

'Shut up, you skinny streak of pus,' Thornton snarled. 'The only reason you tried for Hollinger was for the bounty, not to avenge my son. Billy's biggest mistake was allowing you and Carrow and others like you to get him into trouble.' As Screeby made to protest, Thornton said, 'You got until sundown to get clear of my land. I ever find you near here again I'll kill you myself. You hear me?'

When Screeby hesitated, Mooney said, 'If I was

you I'd get moving.'

After Screeby had scurried out, Sam Mooney went over by the fireplace and pulled out a pipe. He didn't light it, just chewed on it for a bit. He and Nate Thornton went back a long way. He'd known his boss to be wrong-headed before this, but never so wrong as now. He knew the man was ruthless, and he suspected that unlawful and deeply immoral things were sometimes done, but he personally had never been asked to do them. He'd turned away and refused to see what others might be doing. But going up against the law like this, offering money for the murder of a peace officer, and in such a public way, that was bordering on madness.

'What is it, Sam?' Thornton asked. He regarded his foreman with brooding eyes. 'I guess I've known you long enough to know when you ain't saying something you dearly want to get off your chest.'

'All right, boss, I'll say it plain. This don't sit right with me. Putting a bounty on a town marshal is as far over the line as you can go. I know you done some questionable things building this spread and holding on to it, but I always figured maybe they needed doing. I know times were a lot harder when you was setting up, and there weren't much law around, but that's all changed now. What you're doing is going to bring down more trouble than even you can handle.'

Thornton nodded thoughtfully. 'OK Sam, you spoke your piece, and you're right. When I first come out here it was different, sure enough. I fought Shoshoni and Sioux and I lynched rustlers and I buried anyone who stood in my way, and I built this ranch and this business and I became the wealthiest man around. And for what? Who do I leave it to now? My fool wife went and drowned herself in the Snake because she was weak in the head. Couldn't handle neither me nor the life here. She should have stayed back East and married some spineless dandy with water between his legs. Now my only son is dead, murdered in the streets of Bannack, and who have I got left to take over from me?'

'You still have Miss Cordelia,' Mooney reminded him.

Thornton gave an ugly scoffing laugh. 'That's right. I'm blessed with a fool-headed daughter who'll take everything I built and run it into the ground. A daughter who was standing right there defending the man who killed her brother.'

There was silence for a while. Outside, in the hallway, Cord huddled into herself, holding tight to her pain, not wanting to give in to the tears that wanted to be shed. The talk about her mother had awakened old suspicions in her. Suspicions that her mother's death hadn't been an accident.

She was just about to return to her room, her

thoughts and emotions churning in confusion, when she heard her father's angry, hateful voice. 'Each day that passes, news about that bounty will spread to every gunhand in the territory. Ben Hollinger is dead already, he just don't know it yet.'

His words decided her. She'd ride out the first chance she got.

CHAPTER FOUR

THE HUNTERS GATHER

It was Jake Fallon who brought word of the bounty. He rode in from Clearwater a day later. While he stabled his mount he heard all about the gunfight and Leto's death. He rushed headlong into the marshal's office, breathless and disturbed by what he'd heard, and by what he had to tell Hollinger.

'Ten thousand dollars!' he said. 'Word of it is spreading everywhere. There ain't no posters nor nothing, just word of mouth. Someone's paying a bunch of riders to put it about, drifters mostly. What in damnation happened here?'

'Well, I guess that explains Carrow and Screeby,'

Hollinger said. 'I didn't figure them for the sort to risk their lives avenging their friend.' He then brought his deputy up to date on all that had happened.

'I can't believe they killed Leto?' Jake said, still stunned by events in the town. 'I knew there was bad blood between him and Billy Thornton, but I never thought it would lead to a killing. What are you planning on doing, Ben? Thornton has broken the law just by threatening the life of a peace officer, but exactly how we bring him in escapes me. Reese Jackman offered to help, but he's way too old and gimpy for this kind of trouble.'

Hollinger agreed. Jackman was the marshal of Clearwater, but he was well past his prime, although he would never admit to it.

Bracken bustled into the office, looking panicked. 'Marshal, you better take a look out the window.'

'What is it, Doc?'

'Just look over to the saloon. See that feller hitching that big grey to the rail?' Hollinger saw a slim dandy of a man in a pearl-grey frock-coat, with a twirled moustache and sharply pointed beard. A wide-brimmed grey hat, dented in the middle, shaded his eyes, but it was clear he was taking in his surroundings with a coiled wariness before entering the saloon. Two ivory-handled pistols were stuck in a red sash around his waist. 'I swear that's Saul Quist.

41

He matches all the descriptions I've heard.'

Hollinger had heard of Saul Quist. A renowned shootist with a rumoured twenty-three kills to his name, a gun for hire to anyone who could afford him. He looked over towards the office for a moment. A slight smile touched his thin lips before he headed on into the saloon.

'There's no question about why he's here,' Jake said. 'Word of the bounty has sure got around fast.'

'Bounty?' Bracken said. 'What bounty?' After Jake repeated what he'd heard in Clearwater, Bracken spluttered, 'But that's insane! I never heard of such a thing! Thornton can't think he'll get away with that.'

'Losing family in that way, it can make you crazy, Doc.' Hollinger's gaze had turned inwards.

Bracken studied him for a second, before saying gently, 'That was different, Ben, and you know it. The men who killed your family were outlaws on the dodge, lawless murdering scum. They weren't legally appointed lawmen acting in pursuance of their duty.'

Jake said, 'Suppose I go over to the saloon and ask the gentleman to leave town? Unarmed and real polite like. I heard about Quist as well. If he's here for you, he'll try to push you into a shoot-out, but he won't gun down an unarmed man. That would put him outside the law, and Quist is real careful to walk as close inside it as he can.'

It was sound thinking for a peace officer. Avoid violence if at all possible, get any potential trouble out of town as fast as you can. Jake Fallon was no Leto Picken. He was cool-headed and professional. But 10,000 dollars was a hell of a temptation, and Hollinger didn't want his deputy testing Saul Quist's determination to earn it quite so soon.

'Leave him be for the moment,' he said. 'I need time to think this thing through.'

'Just don't be doing any thinking out there on the street,' Bracken snorted. 'I think I'll get Leila to bring your meals over from the saloon. You don't want to be putting temptation in the way of that shootist, or anyone else.'

'I'm the town marshal,' Hollinger protested. 'I can't hide in here, Doc.'

'It's just till we figure this out, see what's best to do. Jake here can do your rounds. There ain't no bounty on his head. I'm going to have a talk with the mayor and Judge Bradley. See if we can't ask the state governor to send in the army until this thing is settled.'

Once Bracken had left, Jake headed out on his patrol. Alone in the office, Hollinger paced restlessly, dark memories surfacing through his sense of anger and frustration, and his feelings of guilt.

*

43

He'd been out tending to the cattle when the band of outlaws had fetched up at his parents' ranch. The first he'd known of it was when the shooting started. He'd ridden back in with two other men. Both had died almost immediately. The only thing that had saved Hollinger was being knocked from his horse as one of the dying men fell against him. His mother had run to him, screaming his name, and he'd seen the bullets hitting her as she ran, hitting her endlessly, until she couldn't run no more. She had died only inches from him.

He'd struggled to his feet, seen his father come running from the ranch house, two handguns blazing away. He'd seen his father fall, and then he'd been knocked unconscious by his panicked cow pony as it reared up, terrified by the gunfire all around it. The outlaws had left him for dead, and he very nearly was. It had been weeks before he was able to ride again.

The seven-man gang had hit a bank three days earlier and had been fleeing a posse. They'd needed fresh mounts and supplies. The slaughter hadn't been necessary, but they'd done it anyway.

The posse never caught up with them, but Ben Hollinger did. It took him almost ten years, but he found them all. Five of them he had killed, and he shuddered now at the memory of what he'd done to two of them. He'd spent so many years with such hatred burning inside him, poisoning his thoughts and his actions. He'd been less than human, until the hunt and the violence eventually sickened him, and he determined to clear himself of its poison.

The last two he hadn't killed. He'd taken them in, and the law had hung them for him. He'd been away from the ranch for a long time, and he couldn't bear the thought of going back. When he was offered work as a deputy sheriff he had accepted. He sold the ranch and became a lawman. He'd moved around a lot since then, ending up in Bannack as the town marshal. It was a peaceful town, the only trouble being an occasional rowdiness from the Tumbling T cowhands. He'd started to believe that the killing was behind him.

But now it was all starting once more. The darkness that had once lain heavy across his soul and that had turned him into an accomplished killer of men, was getting all stirred up again. It was beginning to feel as if those desperate days of bitter hatred and blood-thirsty violence had never gone away.

It was dark when Leila Wendel came, blown in on the gusting rain that had been hammering at the windows for several hours. The hooded cape she wore was shedding rainwater by the barrel-load.

'That is one hell of a night,' she stated. She had a tray of hot food, which was welcome, and news which was not. Besides the shootist, Saul Quist, there was another hunter in town.

'I lived for some years in the Dakota Territory, had me a husband in the cavalry, stationed at Fort Reno.'

'I never knew you were married, Leila.'

'He was killed by the Sioux when he was trying to rescue some settlers, damn fool. But I remember this bounty hunter being around a few times. He was huge, had a big black beard and wore Indian clothes, buckskins and the like. He'd been a mountain man for a while and had lived with the Sioux. I heard it said he'd fought and killed grizzly bears with this big knife he carried. His name was Pardos Leghan, but folks called him Bear Claw on account of this string of claws he had hung around his neck. He was a bounty hunter. And I just seen him in the saloon.'

Hollinger sighed. 'So they're gathering,' was all he said.

'There's been a lot of other folks as well. More drifters than we'd see in a month, saddle tramps mostly, but a few who look a damn sight more dangerous. You have to do something, Ben. This is getting way out of hand. You have to send for help, get the army in here.'

Hollinger knew she was right. He couldn't have armed bands of assassins prowling the streets, waiting for a chance at him. He walked past the

46

window to the right of the door, heading for the coffee pot that was bubbling away on the stove. Leila was still shaking water off her cape when the window beside her exploded inwards. Hollinger ducked low as a volley of rifle shots hammered into the office, one or two ringing loudly off the pot-bellied stove. He felt the hot wind of flying lead above him as he scurried crabwise towards where Leila was standing, just out of the line of fire.

'Leila! Get down!' he yelled.

Leila stood there, rigid with shock, until the marshal pulled her down.

They stayed close to the floor until the shooting stopped, then Hollinger grabbed a shotgun off the rifle rack and flung the door open. Ducking his head clear of the doorframe for a brief second, he saw shadowy figures running along the boardwalk on the far side of the street, past the barbershop with its boarded window. It hadn't been repaired since Tom Carrow had crashed through it.

Further down the street, from the corner of the saloon, he saw brief flashes of flame, and heard the crack-crack of more shots being fired. But they weren't aimed in his direction. He heard Jake Fallon's voice shouting, 'There's two of them, marshal!' Then Jake was running.

Hollinger jumped out into the street, which had become more like a low, fast-flowing river in the last few hours. He splashed across to the opposite board-walk, the water almost up to his knees by the time he got there.

'They went towards the stables!' Jake shouted, as Hollinger came up on him at the corner of the bar-bershop. He was staring through the curtain of rain towards Conover Street.

'Who was it?' Hollinger asked. 'Saul Quist? A big man wearing buckskins?'

'No, it weren't either of those gentlemen. Leila warned me about that Bear Claw feller, but him and Quist is still in the saloon. I was in there keeping an eye on them. There's a lot of strangers in town. It could be any of them.' Jake looked at the marshal. 'If they're in them stables it's gonna be hell getting at them. Are we going in?'

'We are!' Hollinger replied grimly.

Behind them people were beginning to gather, huddled close in the shelter of the covered board-walk. Hollinger turned back to them and shouted, 'You all get way back. There's likely to be some shooting.'

'If there is, that there Greener will sure get it done!' someone shouted back, referring to the marshal's choice of weapon.

Frank Orchin and Dan Backus appeared. Hollinger asked them to keep everyone clear. Both were armed, and Frank said, 'Don't you worry about your back, Ben. We'll make sure no one follows after you.'

As the rain began to ease off Hollinger and his deputy stepped down into the alleyway between the two buildings. Up ahead, on Conover, they could see part of the stable building. They clung to the concealing darkness in the narrow alley until they reached the far end, and had an unobstructed view of the stable doorway.

There was a lantern burning inside, throwing shadows around the cavernous interior. But as they stepped clear of the alley the light went out, and only a gaping maw of darkness waited for them.

'That don't look good,' Jake groaned. 'It's black as hell in there.'

The marshal called out to Frank Orchin and Dan Backus. When they came down the alley he said, 'We need you to put down some covering fire. You have to keep their heads down for a few seconds while we get in there.'

Frank looked at the pitch-dark stables. 'Can't you just wait them out? They got no other way out of there.'

Hollinger shook his head. 'We don't know that they were alone. We have to take them before someone else decides to throw their hand in.'

'Yeah, I guess so,' Frank agreed. He levered a round into his Winchester. 'OK, Dan! Let her rip!'

As the two men laid down a fusillade of rapid fire, Jake and the marshal made their move.

CHAPTER FIVE

GUNS IN THE DARK

Jake and the marshal split to left and right as they rushed the stables. Despite the covering fire guns still flamed from the darkness, bullets slamming into the rear of the barbershop and kicking up mud and rainwater at their feet. They plunged into the shadowed interior with handguns blazing, quickly seeking the protection of a hay-wagon.

A gun-flash from the hayloft betrayed one man's position. The other was over towards the back of the stables, behind a row of stalls, the thunderous reports from his gun driving the horses mad with fear. They were bucking wildly, trying to get loose. Between the darkness and the rearing horses, it was close to impossible to identify a clear target.

Holstering his Colt, the marshal aimed the Greener at a second gun-flash from up above, letting go with both barrels. Accuracy wasn't essential using the shotgun, and he was rewarded with a sharp cry of pain. There was no sound of a falling body, so he figured the gunman wasn't out of action just yet.

'I'll get the other one!' Jake shouted. He waited until the shooting stopped. Hoping that the gunman was reloading he broke cover and hurtled into the deeper shadows of the vast interior, dropping to the ground and rolling behind the wooden planking of a stall halfway along. He had barely reached cover before flying lead began removing wood chunks near his head.

There was no sound or movement from the loft. The upper reaches of the building were black as pitch. Hollinger called out to Jake and the deputy fired a volley of shots up into the darkness, forcing anyone still breathing up there to keep his head down while the marshal ran in under the loft floor. Climbing the ladder would be suicide if the man up there was still a threat.

Hollinger broke open the shotgun and inserted two fresh cartridges, all the while listening for any movement from above. He didn't have long to wait. The wood splintered above his head as slugs hammered down through the flooring. The gunman couldn't be sure of the marshal's position, he was just firing wildly, hoping for a lucky hit.

Hollinger leaped away from the hail of lead, pressing back hard against the wall of the building and letting loose once more with both barrels. Flames flickered into life in the darkness above. Hollinger could see a spreading blaze in the gaps between the wooden planks. Up above him the dry hay had caught fire. In their panic two of the horses got free and galloped madly towards the door of the stables. As the second one ran past him Jake leapt up, unleashing a volley of gunfire while he ran towards the back of the stables.

There was a scream of pain and a gunman staggered out from behind the last stall, lit by the fire burning above. His right shoulder looked shattered, and his gun hand hung useless by his side. Jake slowed as he came up on him and told him to drop the gun.

Above the marshal the fire was spreading rapidly. Burning hay was falling all around him. He looked towards his deputy, who was urging the disarmed gunman towards the front of the stables. 'Get those animals out of here, Jake!' he shouted.

Keeping his prisoner covered while he unlatched the stalls one by one, Jake said, 'Walk on out front, mister, and don't try nothing.' He stepped back as one of the horses reared up, kicking wildly before it galloped for the door. As it thundered past the prisoner he was forced to jump to one side, then he ducked and ran out into the rain-lashed darkness. There was nothing Jake could do about him. Swearing with frustration, he set about freeing the last of the horses and driving them out.

Hollinger moved out from under the loft, getting clear of the fiery rain that fell more heavily with every moment that passed. He shouted over the cracking and snapping of burning wood and the terrified high-pitched screams of the horses, 'Better come down from there, mister. Throw your gun down and then you follow it.'

He heard feet pounding across the floor above him. The gunman was heading for the hayloft door. Dropping the Greener, Hollinger ran outside, into the cold and rain, where he just had time to glimpse Jake's prisoner being held by Frank Orchin and some others. Then he was plunging into the shadows between the stables and the furniture emporium, shadows that were doing a wild dance as flames leapt out from the burning loft.

The second gunman jumped from the hayloft, hit the ground awkwardly, then swung towards the marshal. Hollinger could see where his shotgun blast had peppered the man's left leg, but he was still a threat. He shouted, 'Drop it, mister!'

The man raised his gun arm, firing towards the sound of the marshal's voice. Hollinger's Colt spewed lead, knocking him off his feet with three slugs in his chest. 'Damn fool!' Hollinger muttered, as he stepped over to examine the corpse. He didn't recognize the man, a shabbily dressed drifter by the look of him.

The sounds of shouting and frenzied activity told him that, now the gunfight was over, the town's citizens were turning out to fight the blaze in the stables. As he rejoined Frank Orchin and Jake, he saw a frightened, wounded man cowering between them. He too had the look of a drifter.

'Take him over to the jail,' he told Jake. 'I'll be over once this fire is out.'

'You think that's at all wise?' a voice asked from behind him. He turned to see Bracken standing there, concern on his wrinkled brow. 'Those fellers won't be the only ones eager to earn that bounty. You don't want to make yourself an easy target, Ben. If I was you I'd leave the fire to the good citizens of this town and I'd get the hell off the street as fast as I could.'

Hollinger looked around him, at the many strangers mingling with the townsfolk. A great many eyes were turned on him. He saw the wisdom in the doctor's words.

'OK,' he said. 'Tell me when the fire's under control.'

As he and Jake escorted their prisoner back to the

office he was aware of an armed escort at their backs. Frank Orchin, Dan Backus and a couple of others were carrying rifles, seeing the marshal back to safety.

Towards dawn the rain eased a bit. Hollinger sat at his desk with Jake, Frank and Dan all pacing around him. Frank and Dan kept a watch through the windows, the shattered one allowing damp air into the office.

'I have to leave town before this gets any worse,' Hollinger told them. 'I can't put people at risk by having pitched battles right out there in the street.'

Bracken came out of the back room, towelling his hands dry. There were two jail cells in there, and the wounded drifter was in one of them. They'd got his name out of him, Hollis, but not much more. The dead one was called Spence. They'd heard about the bounty over in a nearby town called Willow Creek, and had figured on trying their luck.

'How is he, Doc?' Hollinger asked.

'He'll live. Shoulder's broke, but he should be mighty thankful he's still breathing. That was good shooting, Jake, especially in the dark.'

'It was dumb luck. I was just blasting away at him.'

Bracken turned to the marshal. 'What's that about you leaving town? Out in the open you'll make a much easier target.'

'Out in the open I'll have a better chance of seeing them coming. I do have some experience with this kind of thing. Remember?'

Bracken did indeed remember. He was one of the few people who knew the details of Ben Hollinger's past. He gave the marshal a troubled look. 'Yeah, I guess you do at that. OK, you got a point there.'

'I'm coming with you,' Jake said.

'No, you're staying right here. This town still needs a lawman, especially when we got all them strangers drifting in. You got Frank and Dan to back you up. If you boys don't mind lending a hand, I'll deputize you both.'

'You do that, Marshal,' Frank said. 'I don't figure on allowing no saddle bums to make more trouble than we already got.'

'Where are you planning on going?' Bracken asked.

'The old Warren place, up in the hills.'

Bracken knew it. A broken down ranch house, barn and stables, all overgrown and derelict. The Warrens had never had much, but they had land that Nate Thornton had wanted. He'd never been one to tolerate neighbours, especially other ranchers, and especially a small operation like the Warrens' Circle W. He'd bought them out after a short campaign of intimidation and harassment, and the Warrens had been only too happy to go.

'That's across the river, but it's still on Tumbling T land,' Bracken cautioned.

'But a little corner of it that they only use during round-up,' Hollinger said. 'Everyone will figure on me staying clear of Thornton's property, and I got the beginnings of an idea on how to end this.'

'Is it an idea I'd feel at all comfortable with?' Bracken asked, frowning at what he knew the answer would be.

Hollinger smiled grimly. 'I don't think so, but I don't have a whole lot of choices.'

'You could call in the army. Tell the state governor about Thornton's bounty.'

Frank shook his head. 'I talked to the mayor earlier. He was planning on asking for help, but somebody's pulled the telegraph wires down. Somewhere between here and Clearwater. I think we can all guess who. He's sending a rider out. I think young Jed Lowry has volunteered.'

'That'll take time,' Hollinger said. 'Time we don't have if this town is going to avoid a bloodbath. I'm leaving you to notify the governor, but I'm pulling out now. With any luck all the bounty hunters around town will light out after me.'

'That don't seem like any kind of luck,' Frank said.

'It's the only play I got,' Hollinger told him.

Bracken sighed. 'I'd suggest one or more of us

senior citizens going out to the ranch to talk some sense into Nate Thornton, except I don't see he's got much sense left. I spent the best part of my life in this town, and I can tell you he was always mean and cruel and ruthless to a degree that was less than human. But since his wife killed herself he's added crazy-mad to that little list of dubious virtues.'

'Killed herself?' Hollinger was startled. 'I heard rumours, but I thought they were just that, idle wagging tongues that like to make mischief. She drowned in the Snake, didn't she?'

Bracken nodded. 'Maybe it was an accident, maybe not. I tend to think that when a woman is suffering like Lisa Thornton was, then the wagging tongues might have got it right for once. Like I said, Nate Thornton was always a cruel man, and for a gentle young woman like Lisa, married to a much older man who treated her like a personal possession, it might have proved too much.'

Hollinger thought of Cord, and wondered how much she knew about her mother's drowning. Was that why she rarely mentioned her?

'Old man Thornton's as bad as they come,' Frank added. 'There hasn't been so much trouble since you took over as marshal here, but before that we had other ranch owners complaining about Thornton's tactics. About two years ago a bunch of free-grazers disappeared off the face of the earth.

Some people came looking for them, but they was never found. Last place they'd been seen was on Tumbling T land.'

'I can't believe that Sam Mooney would be in on that,' Hollinger said. He had some respect for the ranch foreman, who seemed like a decent man.

'I don't think Mooney gets told everything,' Frank said.

'Sun's coming up,' Dan Backus told them. He was still standing over by the broken window, keeping watch.

'Then I better ride,' the marshal said.

Ten minutes later he was mounted on the big dapple-grey, his deputies spread out across the street, rifles ready for any sign of trouble. Of those who saw him ride out of Bannack there were six who eased out of sight of the armed deputies, slipping down back streets and mounting their own horses. Hollinger had hardly cleared the town limits before they were on his trail.

CHAPTER SIX

RIVER CROSSING

By noon Hollinger had reached the Snake. At this particular spot, in late summer and early autumn, the low water made fording the river much less dangerous. He'd heard of folks being swept away when the river was high and running fast. Lisa Thornton was supposed to have been one of those unfortunates, but from what Bracken had told him, that was open to debate. There was a ferry downstream, operated by an old-timer called Edgar O'Rourke, but it was an obvious place for an ambush, should anyone have seen the trail he took out of town.

He and Miles Bracken had done some fishing here during the summer, for rainbow trout. The doctor had been the first to befriend him when he'd arrived in Bannack, and had gone out of his way to support the new marshal. He liked the old man. He reminded him of his father in his quiet manner, his dry humour, and his sensible nature. He'd gone fishing with his father too, and the sudden memory brought the bitter taste of hatred with it. He'd lived for too long with that hatred burning inside him, even after the men who'd murdered his family were dead and under the dirt. His years as a lawman had softened it some, had turned his thirst for revenge into a dedication to uphold the law, and to protect others from suffering the same fate as his family.

He shuddered at the unbidden memory of first his mother, then his father falling under a hail of bullets. He still heard the dull slap of the slugs hitting, hitting, hitting. It took for ever for his mother to fall, or so it seemed to him, and while she fell the outlaws laughed and jeered. He thought of Sasha Barlow's kids, seeing their mother gunned down, and the old dark feelings and urges began to rise in him. Then he thought, was he any better than those killers he'd put down? He'd gunned down Billy Thornton, no more than a boy, right in front of his sister.

His thoughts darkening, he urged the big dapple-grey into the shallow water. There was trailing moss on the river bed, the clear water caressing it like a gentle lover. On the other side, beyond the rocks and boulders, the land rose steeply into a cover of green pine and fir trees. He was safely across and riding up into the protective shadows when he heard the drumming of hoofs from behind him.

He dismounted quickly, slipped his Winchester rifle from the saddle and took cover behind a fallen pine tree. There were six riders. It was clear that none of them was a professional. They galloped down to the river without any caution at all, certain that their numbers gave them the advantage over the one lone man who was their prey. That was a mistake that would cost them some blood.

They studied the river for a few moments, while one of their number circled his horse around the churned-up mud left by the dapple-grey.

'He crossed here!' the man shouted. 'Not too long ago. I reckon we're just minutes behind him.'

One of the others, a ruddy-faced man in a stovepipe hat and long duster, gave a Rebel yell, as though the prize was already won. His pleasure didn't last more than a second. A bullet from Hollinger's Winchester sent the hat flying off his head.

Someone shouted to take cover, but there was no real cover to be had on that side of the river, not if they wanted to be within shooting distance of their prey. A volley of shots from the Winchester sent them scurrying back, the horses panicking as badly as the men riding them as bullets kicked up dirt around their hoofs. Two of the riders fell, thrown by their mounts.

More saddle tramps, Hollinger reckoned. They were looking for easy money. They'd be easily discouraged if they really had to work at earning it, and maybe chance dying in the attempt. They'd give up once they saw that the odds weren't completely stacked in their favour. Except for two of them: the two who pulled their guns and came charging across the river, yelling and firing wildly as they came.

Hollinger reloaded. The first one was almost clear of the river when a bullet from the Winchester knocked him out of the saddle. He fell with a noisy splash and the water churned red with his death throes. The second man was the one who'd lost the stovepipe hat. He threw himself off his horse and dived behind the rocks.

Hollinger waited, but Stovepipe refused to show himself. He was crouched low, moving among the rocks. Even though he was out of sight, the marshal followed his progress easily. One of the men on the far bank had fled, but the remaining three were watching Stovepipe, giving away his changing position without realizing it. Hollinger smiled to himself, wondering at the foolishness of such men. But he couldn't wait all day for Stovepipe to show himself. There was no telling how many others might join in the pursuit. He'd have to lure him out into the open, and fast.

He bellied backwards, away from the fallen pine, and went back to the dapple-grey. He undid the tether and slapped its rump. It galloped off a little way, and Hollinger got back to the fallen tree in time to see Stovepipe breaking cover, clearly under the impression that the marshal was running. He only discovered his mistake when Hollinger's rifle barked out once more, and a bullet tore open his chest. As he flopped backwards on to the rocks the other three broke and ran. The marshal sent a couple of rounds after them by way of encouragement. Not that they needed it.

The dapple-grey had run only a little way off. It had been through such battles before. It came cantering back in response to Hollinger's whistle. As he stowed the rifle and hoisted himself into the saddle, the marshal took a grim-faced look back at the bloodied river. He'd thought he'd left such killings behind, that the vengeance trail he'd ridden for so many years had come to an end. But now he was both hunter and hunted once more, caught in the cycle of revenge, the dance of death he'd proved so good at.

This time a man wanted payment of him, for the death of a loved one at Hollinger's hands. That he could understand. The hatred Nate Thornton felt towards him was the same as he'd felt for those outlaws who'd murdered his family. That he was a lawman doing his duty wouldn't enter into it, he knew that. To Thornton he was just the man who'd killed his son.

For his part, Hollinger knew that he had to exact payment for Leto Picken. It was his job as a peace officer to bring Thornton in. He shouldn't be motivated by any personal need for revenge over his deputy's death, and yet the coldness inside him, the ruthless determination to bring a grieving father to justice, felt no different to him from the years of pursuing desperate killers.

More men were going to die before this was over, that was certain. Perhaps the marshal himself. But he wouldn't go easy, and he would take some with him, including Nate Thornton.

With a last look towards the river, he urged the dapple-grey on up the slope. Hopefully the rocky ground would leave little evidence of his passing, but an experienced tracker would find him eventually. His stay at the Warren ranch had to be brief, and he had to have a plan in place before he left again.

Nate Thornton had said that no one else was to leave the ranch, but someone clearly wasn't too intent on obeying that order. Seeing who was riding the pinto, Sam Mooney urged his cow pony into a gallop that brought him alongside Thornton's daughter.

'Cord, where in hell are you going?'

'Into town.'

'Into town? Are you plumb crazy? With all that's happened, you think the townsfolk are gonna give anyone from the Tumbling T a warm welcome?' Cord kept on riding and he snapped, 'Cord! Hold up a goddamn minute!'

Cord reined in, turning a grim and determined face on him. 'Someone has to do something, Sam.'

'And what can you do, Missy?' Since she was a child, Cord had always been called Missy by the ranch hands she was particularly friendly with. The ones who had worked the ranch for a long time were like family. Her father didn't see it that way, as he'd proved in the past, but Cord did.

'I don't know, Sam. I don't know that I can do anything. All I know is, I have to try. A young woman died, a mother, because of my father's insane bounty. He doesn't care who gets hurt next, but I do. I won't sit back and do nothing. I can't.'

Mooney studied her for a moment. His voice softened when he said, 'I know you can't. All right, Missy, you go do whatever you can. I never saw you go.'

He watched until she was out of sight, a drift of trail dust the only sign of her passing.

*

By the time the four bedraggled and frightened-looking riders got back to town, the Remuda saloon was playing host to another arrival. A dark-skinned man with startling blue eyes that looked like they could punch holes in human flesh, he wore the clothing of a Mexican *vaquero* and carried a hunting rifle. He pushed through the batwing doors and stood for a moment, his piercing gaze raking the room before it settled on the furthest table, where Pardos Leghan sat alone.

Jake Fallon and Dan Backus were in the saloon, keeping a watch on both Quist and Leghan. Backus drew in a breath as he saw the newcomer crossing the room. 'Hell! You know who that is?'

'Never seen him before. Who is he?'

'His name's Riley Alvarez. Half Mexican and half Irish, and all pure downright meanness. Another bounty hunter. They say he's the best tracker in the business. Him and Bear Claw have partnered up before, and they're a lethal match. The marshal's troubles just got a lot worse. Wherever he's gone those two will find him, don't matter how well he's covered his tracks.'

Jake watched with a worried gaze as Alvarez went over to Leghan's table.

Tossing his sombrero down, the Mexican pulled up a chair. He sat with his rifle cradled in both arms. Leghan glanced at the Remington-Rider rolling-block hunting rifle and said, 'You took your time getting here.'

'My apologies, *hombre*. Didn't get your message until late yesterday. I hear the marshal has left town.'

'He done a jackrabbit all right. Bunch of idiots went out after him.' Leghan looked over towards the door as the remnants of the hunting party staggered in. 'I guess that's what's left of them. Looks like they got shot to hell. I heard about this lawman. He's the same Ben Hollinger as hunted down the Riker gang a few years ago. It don't do to underestimate him. He's got a reputation, well deserved by all accounts.'

Alvarez scowled. 'Word of this bounty has spread all over the territory. If we don't move fast we could get trampled in the stampede, or killed in the cross-fire.'

Leghan's teeth showed in the depths of his beard, bared in a savage grin. 'We leave right now. I got all the provisions we need, but I ain't expecting a long hunt. This is Hollinger's town, he ain't gonna be too far away.'

As they headed for the door, one of the hunting party, slumped over the long bar counter with a whiskey in his hand, turned to stare at Alvarez.

Alvarez stopped, stared back. 'You think you know me, *hombre?*'

The man dropped his gaze. 'I heard of you. You're that Mexican bounty hunter. I hear tell you're a dead shot with that thing.' He pointed at the rifle.

'You didn't hear it from anyone I've shot at,' Alvarez replied. A chilling smile touched his lips, but got nowhere near his startling blue eyes.

Cordelia Thornton arrived in town just as the two bounty hunters were riding out. On being told that the marshal had gone, and that the Bannack citizens' committee was having an emergency meeting in a top-floor room of the courthouse, she headed straight up.

As she entered the room she heard Frank Orchin demanding that a posse be deputized and sent out to the Tumbling T with a warrant for Nate Thornton's arrest. Leila Wendel was backing him up, and insisting on organizing a defence of the town.

Judge Bradley was presiding, as always. He was a small, distinguished-looking man with flyaway wings of white hair above his temples. 'What do you think of that suggestion Mr Bell?' he asked. 'You think your client is likely to come quietly?'

Hamilton Bell sat a little to one side, confusion and panic clear in his eyes. Nate Thornton's downfall would be his own, but his position in the community was also in jeopardy, if it was discovered that it was he who had paid the drifters who spread word of Thornton's bounty. He shook his head sadly. 'No I don't. I think that a posse riding on to

Tumbling T land will only start a war.'

'The hell with that!' Frank Orchin shouted. 'Have you looked at the streets of our town. We already have a war out there.'

Miles Bracken, who had been listening carefully to the arguments, noticed Cord for the first time, standing over by the door looking scared and uncertain. He spoke her name and everyone in the room turned her way.

Someone shouted, 'That's his daughter! Ask her how far her father's going to take this. How many people is he going to have murdered on the streets of Bannack?'

Cord looked around the mostly hostile faces, then she turned and fled. As she clattered down the stairs she heard Bracken's voice calling from above, 'Cordelia! Please! Wait up, girl!'

She stopped by the entrance, allowing Bracken to catch up. 'Good lord, girl! What are you doing in town?' he said breathlessly. 'Feelings are running high. You could be putting yourself in harm's way.'

'I'm not the only one. Oh, Doc! Ben is in terrible danger. My father—'

'Yes, I know. We all know about the bounty. There's been some killings already.'

'Ben! Is he. . . ?'

'No, Ben's all right, for the moment. But I guess you know that Leto is dead, and a young woman called Sasha Barlow, who was shot by Tom Carrow.'

Cord nodded. 'Screeby told us about Leto, and then Hamilton Bell brought us news about the woman. I'm so sorry, Doc. I can't stop thinking about her poor children.'

'Your father's got some charges to answer, when the marshal catches up to him.'

'Catches up to him?' Cord paled as she took in the full meaning of Bracken's words. 'Ben's going after my father? He has a posse?'

Bracken shook his head. 'No posse.'

'He couldn't be crazy enough to try taking him at the ranch, all by himself. That'd be suicide. My father has a small army out there. I don't know that they'd all back him in this madness he's started, but there's a few who might. They wouldn't go against him at any rate. Ben wouldn't stand a chance alone. I've got to talk to him. Where is he?'

'He's already gone. Left town this morning.'

'Going where?'

Bracken shifted uneasily. 'Come on, Cordelia. I can't tell you that.'

Cord looked at him, astonishment and a growing anger sparking in her eyes. 'Why? Because I'm Nate Thornton's daughter, and my daddy wants the marshal dead? You think I feel the same way, Doc?'

'The way I heard it, you were pretty upset in the saloon, after Ben was forced to kill your brother. You called him a murderer.'

Cord drew in a deep breath, then let it out slowly. 'I was upset, sure enough. I saw my brother shot to death and I blamed the man who shot him. I behaved like a fool, Doc. I know that Ben had no choice. I know it wasn't murder. Billy might have killed me if he'd got off another shot.' She touched the still livid marks on her face. 'I was standing right behind the marshal, but that made no never mind to my brother. I knew Billy was bad. I always knew. I saw more of his cruelty and wickedness than my father ever did. He didn't care about nobody but himself. His manner and his behaviour were always going to get him killed, sooner or later.'

'Ben would have preferred that it be later, and by someone else,' Bracken said.

'So would I, but that can't be helped now. If Ben is planning on taking my father he's going to need help. Where did he go, Doc? Please! You have to tell me!'

Bracken thought it over for a moment. Fear and desperation were clear to see in Cordelia Thornton's eyes. He made his decision, and then they made a plan.

CHAPTER SEVEN

A PLACE FOR CROWS

The old Warren place was cradled in a depression between two ridges of high ground. Having circled the depression once, Hollinger rode in. It looked unoccupied. He'd seen nothing but some big black crows settled on the broken-down fencing and the roofs of the deserted house, barn and stables.

He led the dapple-grey into the stables, which were to the rear of the house, then went to draw some water from the nearby well. The barn was close by the stables, part of its roof and its west wall all collapsed inwards. He tended to the dapple-grey, then took a look around. As he walked between the wood-frame buildings the crows took off, screeching their defiance to the darkening sky. They didn't much take to intruders.

Heavy clouds were rolling in, threatening to bring the dusk an hour or two early. It was getting cold. The marshal shrugged into the sheepskin coat he had tied over the saddle, heaved his saddle-bags over one shoulder, grabbed the Winchester and headed for the house. He planned on getting a fire started, get some food in him, and then think about what his next move was going to be.

My next move, he thought to himself. Probably suicide, but his choices were limited, if he didn't want to spend the next few years running from every fool with a gun and enough greed in him to risk his life. Getting to Nate Thornton was the only way he could see of stopping all this, but it wasn't going to be easy.

The front door of the house was warped and half-hanging from rusted hinges. He pushed it wide with his foot, and had just stepped over the threshold when he heard the creak of wood under someone's boot. He wasn't alone. He dropped the saddle-bags and started to bring the rifle up, but a harsh whispery voice stopped him.

'You'll never make it, marshal! I got you dead to rights! Damned if I don't!'

Hollinger froze, turning his head in the direction

of the voice. The interior of the house was gloomy, dark shadows everywhere. A badly made stone chimney, stained black from repeated fires, dominated the main living area, with doorways on each side of it leading to other rooms. It was stripped of furniture, which the Warrens had taken with them when they pulled out. It took a second to locate the source of the voice, a ragged scarecrow-like shadow standing over on the far side of the fireplace.

'Screeby!' Hollinger hissed, angry with himself that he had failed to spot the man's presence. He looked at the rifle aimed towards his gut, a Sharps carbine, and knew that he hadn't a prayer.

'Well now, looky here,' Screeby drawled. As Hollinger lowered the arm holding the Winchester, his tone relaxed into one of easy confidence. 'If it ain't the murderin' law dog hisself. I reckon Mr Thornton's gonna be right happy to welcome me back, when he sees what I brung him.'

Hollinger said, 'You figure on claiming the bounty?'

'Well now, I don't rightly see what's to stop me. I seen you riding about up there in the rocks for quite a while, deciding whether there was anyone here. So I stayed hid and waited. I been hiding out here since Thornton kicked me out. He weren't too happy that me and Carrow didn't kill you in town, but I'll get the job done now.' Screeby stepped forward, ready to shoot. A board, rotted right through, snapped under his heel and he staggered, the shot going wide and clipping the marshal's ear.

Hollinger ducked low, feeling hot blood on the side of his face as he brought the Winchester up and fired. He saw Screeby lurch back under the impact, levered another round into the chamber and fired again. The second slug slammed into Screeby's face, tearing a hole where his nose had been and leaving a bloody, gaping maw. He hit the ground and the floorboards gave way under him.

Hollinger moved cautiously across the floor, the warped boards creaking uneasily under his boot-heels. He stared into the darkness of the hole Screeby's body had made, seeing dead black eyes in a pale, noseless face. The mouth was still stretched wide in a last dying scream. The marshal shuddered, his body reacting to the closeness of death. Not just at Screeby's death, but what had very nearly been his own.

In the gathering darkness he stanched the wound to his ear. It was slight, but bleeding like the devil. Then he lit the few lanterns that still hung around the place, those that still had oil in them to burn. He gathered Screeby's body up out of the floor, covered it in an old rotted horse-blanket he found in the stables, and left it lying in the barn. He'd bury him in the morning, but first he needed a fire and some food. The house wasn't safe, but there was a little room at the rear of the stables, probably intended to house any help the Warrens might have hired. It had a stove in there, and a bunk that seemed comfortable enough. It was obvious that Screeby had put up there, only entering the house to ambush the marshal.

Sitting before the lit stove an hour later, with food warming his belly, he had time to brood on what tomorrow would bring. He'd covered his tracks well, but given enough time any expert trackers would find him. He couldn't move against Thornton in daylight. Even in the dark the Tumbling T would be well defended, but it was his only chance. To get to Nate Thornton before he was discovered and gunned down would require not only the stealth he had learned during those long years on the vengeance trail, it would take a great deal of luck. His chances weren't great, but it was his only play.

When at last he slipped into a light sleep, part of him still alert for any unusual noises out in the night, his dreams were uneasy. He dreamed of the men he had killed, and who had almost killed him. He heard their dying screams and saw their dead eyes watching him, waiting for him to join them in their dark little corner of hell.

He dreamed too of Cordelia Thornton. He had dreamed of her many times before, of her curling honey-blonde hair and green eyes, of her ripe curves and wayward nature. He had always awakened feeling slightly foolish and ashamed of his desire for her, a desire that was only fully acknowledged by his sleeping mind. Cord had made her feelings known to him early on, and in far too forward a manner for his liking. But that was her way. When she wanted something she went after it. Her father and her brother had never shown her any other way.

Hollinger was attracted to her, but it was a pairing that could never be. Cord was way too young to waste her life on a troubled, conscience-stricken killer of men. She was a rich man's daughter, and he was a lawman who earned a few dollars a week, food and board. Besides, Nate Thornton would never have allowed it, even before the marshal killed his only son.

He dreamed of Cordelia Thornton, but this time he saw the hate in her eyes as he stood over her dead brother. In his sleep his face twisted in pain, the guilt stabbing at him like knives.

It was early, an hour before dawn, when Cord drove the wagon up to the ferry crossing, her own mount tied on behind. Edgar O'Rourke saw her through the window of his cabin and hurried out, swearing loudly and attempting to pull his braces up.

'Darned useless things! Never can get them the

right way!' He squinted through eyes that were still blurred with sleep. 'Unless I'm much mistaken, that's Miss Cordelia Thornton I see perched up there on that wagon. The question is, what the hell is Miss Cordelia Thornton doing out here at this ungodly hour?'

'She has a favour to ask,' Cord told him.

'A favour!' O'Rourke spluttered. 'This early in the day?'

'I need your help, and so does the marshal.'

O'Rourke calmed down. He gave Cord a sharply perceptive look. 'Ah yes, the marshal. I had me some right interesting visitors yesterday. They staked out the ferry most of the day, waiting for the marshal to show, like he'd be that foolish. You got me all curious now. What you got in mind?'

While Cord was telling him, the old man stood and scratched both at his nether regions and at his scraggly white beard. By the time she was finished, he was grinning like some mischievous old devil just up out of hell.

'You got some sand for a little bitty snip of a thing,' he cackled. 'Your own father too. But he needs stopping, sure enough. I heard about the killings in town, and I got no sympathy for them that does harm to women or children. You tell the marshal if he needs help I'll be right proud to ride with him. My hands shake a mite, and my eyes ain't so good, but I reckon I can still hold my old Greener, and it don't discriminate overmuch, once you let loose in the right direction.'

'I'll tell him,' Cord said, smiling to herself.

Leaving the wagon, she led her pinto on to the ferry. O'Rourke took her across and watched as she rode up into the hills, then he headed back across the river.

'Some folks got a big surprise coming,' he cackled.

Riley Alvarez had taken his position in the rocks before dawn. He was used to waiting for his prey, for that one perfect shot that was all he needed. The Remington-Rider rolling-block rifle was on the rocks beside him.

The rifle had a strong action, but wasn't that fast to operate. He wanted to be loaded and ready. Once he'd settled on where to shoot from, he'd cocked the hammer, freeing the pivoted breechblock. Then he'd thumbed the rolling block backward and down to reveal the cartridge chamber, which was empty. He'd slipped a cartridge in and rolled the breech-block up to seal the chamber, then eased the hammer to half-cock for safety. He was ready. All he needed was a target, but it was another three hours before Ben Hollinger obliged him by stepping into the open.

Alvarez raised the iron sights and drew a bead on the marshal, as he hauled a blanket-covered shape out of the stables. He went back in and emerged a moment later with a spade. Alvarez guessed that the shape was a dead body, and that the marshal was intent on burying it. He sure had been busy since leaving town.

He waited until Hollinger chose a spot and began digging. He wet his thumb and held it up, checking the direction and strength of the wind. Finally, he sighted in on his target and eased the hammer to full cock, his mouth twisting into a tight smile. This was the moment he lived for, when he gently squeezed the exposed hammer, which was placed behind the breechblock, and watched the impact of his bullet as it hit the target.

At that moment, all thoughts about the $10,000 were emptied from his head. He was given over completely to the shot he was about to make. His pleasure in killing was unconnected to any reward. His smile was one of sheer unholy joy, as he squeezed the trigger and the rifle bucked against his shoulder.

Pain jolted through him as he saw the marshal drop.

CHAPTER EIGHT

THREE GRAVES

Hollinger dropped to the ground, drawing his Colt as the hard earth took the breath from his lungs. Dirt was kicked up only inches away. There had been two shots, so close together that they'd almost sounded like one. A moment later a third shot was fired, but it didn't seem to be aimed at him. At least one of those first two shots certainly had been. Not knowing who was doing the shooting, the marshal scrambled to his feet and ran for the stables.

His Winchester was sitting by one of the stalls, but he never got to it. As he ran into the building a massive arm the size of a tree trunk sprang up in front of him. Seeing it at the last moment, Hollinger knew that he had too much speed to stop. He tried

83

to duck under the arm, but a fist like a falling anvil crashed down on his right shoulder, numbing it instantly.

He fell to the ground, rolled, and came up again, just as his attacker jumped him from behind. The tree-trunk arm wrapped itself around his throat, choking him as it tightened. He grabbed at the arm, fighting for breath, and saw the other hand come down over his numbed right shoulder, driving a huge hunting knife towards his chest. It looked to be half the size of a cavalry sabre. He reached across with his left hand, seizing his attacker's wrist in a desperate attempt to halt the downward motion of the blade.

Now he knew who his assailant was. The knife and the sleeve of a buckskin coat, plus the man's sheer size, told him it was Pardos Leghan. The fearsome Bear Claw! A man who claimed to have fought and killed grizzly bears in hand-to-claw combat. One puny human being shouldn't give him too much trouble. Despite his best efforts, the knife continued its slow but unstoppable downward arc, inching towards Hollinger's chest. He knew that matching his strength against that of the mountain man was useless.

Drawing up his left foot he drove his boot-heel down hard along Leghan's shinbone and into his foot. The mountain man grunted, but was otherwise unmoved. Their struggle had brought them near one of the horse stalls, and as the marshal felt his grip on Leghan's knife hand weaken, he lifted both feet and kicked hard against the wooden stall. The impact threw both him and his assailant backwards. He felt the pressure on his throat ease a little as the mountain man staggered, tried to regain his balance. Hollinger snapped his head back, felt the springiness of Leghan's beard as he connected with his chin. They fell backwards, Leghan still trying to hold on to him. His choking arm hold had loosened too much, and the marshal rolled clear as they hit the ground, but it was only for a moment.

With a speed that was amazing, given the man's bulk, Leghan was on him again, slamming him against the stall. Once again Hollinger managed to stop the knife that was sweeping down towards his chest, but Leghan clamped the other hand to his windpipe, slowly crushing the life from him. Either the knife or the huge hand was about to end his life, and the marshal was trapped against the wooden stall. As his senses began to swirl and spin, the bear-claw necklace seemed to dance before his eyes.

Leghan was a head taller than the marshal, and he was so close that the foulness of his breath was almost suffocating. Hollinger looked up and saw the killing lust in Leghan's murderous, red-eyed stare and he saw his death written plainly there. In one final desperate act he raised his weakened right arm and grabbed the necklace, driving one of the claws as deep and as hard as he could into the mountain man's left eye.

Leghan screamed and staggered back, away from the bloodied claw. As he clutched at his gouged eye-socket Hollinger seized the hand holding the knife and drove the wide blade into the man's gut. Even that didn't bring the giant down. Still howling in agony, with blood flowing down his face from his ruined eye, the half-blind mountain man pulled the blade free of his own belly and advanced once more on the marshal.

'Jesus God!' Hollinger breathed, as he watched the monster come at him again.

The Winchester was near by, resting against a stall. He pumped its entire load into the mountain man before Leghan at last sank to his knees, sitting for a moment with a look of disbelief on his face, then he fell with a crash that shook the building.

'Ben?' A tremulous voice came from the doorway.

Hollinger turned to see Cordelia Thornton stand-ing there, a rifle in her hands and a look of dismay on her bloodless face. She looked from the moun-tain man's vast corpse to the blood-soaked marshal. For a second Hollinger wondered whether she was going to turn the rifle on him, but when she spoke he understood that he might live a little longer. Had she raised the rifle and taken aim, he knew he couldn't have returned her fire. He'd have taken her bullet before doing any harm to her.

'Oh, Ben! Thank the Lord! I thought that man in the rocks had killed you! I saw you fall!'

She dropped the rifle and ran to him. Hollinger winced as she closed her arms around him, his right arm protesting. He stood frozen for a moment, unsure of how to react, then he put his still good left arm around her waist. She felt soft and firm at the same time, and the scent of her honey-blonde hair was intoxicating to a man who had been so nearly a corpse but a few moments earlier.

'Cord,' he murmured, trying to get his balance. He had never been this close to her before, had never embraced her before, and he wasn't sure how it had happened now, when she was supposed to hate him. 'I would have figured you for giving them a hand. Last time I saw you, you were fixing to kill me yourself.'

Her soft green eyes were pleading as she replied, 'I never meant it, Ben. Never! I saw my brother die and I was crazy mad at you. But I know he gave you no choice. He'd have maybe killed me as well if he'd got off another shot. He was rotten right through, but he was my brother. I'm so sorry for the way I acted, and now my father—'

'You don't have to apologize for what happened,

Cord. I wouldn't blame you for hating me. If I could change it I would. I didn't want to kill Billy. I didn't want to cause you and your pappy so much pain. I know what it is to lose loved ones in that way.'

'But I don't hate you, Ben. You have to know that. I tried to tell my father what happened, but he wouldn't listen. Now all these people are dead and I. . . .' She lowered her head and sobbed into his chest for a bit.

Hollinger held her, letting her get it all out. He'd always avoided touching her, afraid that the way he felt about her would show too clearly. He hadn't wanted her to think that her attentions towards him were in any way welcome. She was too young, too pretty, and too rich for a killer earning a town marshal's pay.

Very gently, he lifted her hands away and said, 'Who was shooting up in the rocks?'

Cord shook her head. 'I don't know. A bounty hunter I guess. Mexican, maybe. I saw him from a ways off. I wanted to make sure you were here before riding in, and that nobody else was, so I came up in back of the house. You couldn't have spotted him, but he was visible from where I was. I dismounted pretty far back, and came up behind him. When I saw him fixing to shoot, I opened fire. Got him in the shoulder with a lucky shot, just as he loosed off on you. He twisted around, tried to shoot back at

88

me, so I put a second slug in him. He's dead.'

'It would have been me, if you hadn't come along.'

'When I saw you fall I thought he'd killed you. Then, after I shot him again, you'd disappeared. I couldn't see where you'd gone to. As I came closer I heard sounds from in here, knew someone was fighting. I saw the last of it. He didn't die easy.'

'I didn't think he was going to die at all. But why are you here, Cord? How did you find me?'

'Doc told me.'

'Doc?'

'He trusted me, Ben. He knows how I feel about you, even better than you do. He told me what you're intent on doing. You'll never pull it off, you know that? Not without help, and that's why I'm here.'

Hollinger took a step back, looking grim. 'Cord, I intend to arrest your pappy. I got no other choice, no other way to stop this. You're going to go up against your own father to help me?'

'People have been killed. That young woman, and Leto. My father or not, I can't let things like that happen. Me and Doc, we worked out a plan.'

'You and Doc?' A slight smile creased his lips.

'Me and Doc,' she said defiantly. 'Why are you smiling? You think we can't work out a plan? What were you going to do? Ride in shooting and hope for the best?'

'I might have been a bit more subtle.' The smile widened into an appreciative grin. 'God, but you're feisty!'

Cord planted her hands on her hips and said, 'Do you want to hear this plan or not?'

'Sure I do.'

'OK then. I left Bannack before sunrise, so no one would see me go, with a wagon full of supplies. Frank and Jenny Orchin helped with that part.'

'Supplies? Why would I need supplies?'

'You don't. I left the wagon down by the ferry, came up here on my pony. Now, if you want to hush up and listen to me, I'll tell you what they're for.'

So the marshal hushed up, and Cord told him.

They had a meal in back of the stables, from the small makings that Hollinger had brought with him. Cord told him about Edgar O'Rourke and his offer of help.

Hollinger smiled. 'That old man's as full of vinegar as they come.'

'So, you think the plan will work?' Cord asked him.

'I think it's the best one we have. You and Doc could teach strategy to the army.'

'Thank you kindly. It's nice to be appreciated. All right, so we put up here for most of the day, then I'll go get the wagon and you meet me where I said.

90

Upstream from the ferry, where there's a lot of cover. I want it to be close to sundown before I take the wagon in. We got a better chance in the dark.'

'I'm still not happy about your part in this,' Hollinger said.

They were sitting on a horse-blanket that Hollinger had thrown over the bunk. The remains of their meal sat close by. Neither of them had shown much appetite. Cord gave the marshal a level look and said, 'This is the best chance you got. Maybe the only one. You can't talk me out of it, so don't try.'

'You made that more than clear. But you'll allow me to worry.'

She touched the side of his face, which was still raw from the wood splinters that Bracken had extracted. 'I think it's you who needs taking care of, not me. You're a mess. What happened to your ear? It's all dried blood.'

'I had to evict a previous tenant. You got a little peppered there yourself.' He pointed to the pin-prick scars still showing on Cord's face.

She fell silent for a moment, before speaking in a quiet, serious voice. 'I could have been shot as well, maybe killed. You maybe saved both our lives when you shot Billy. I want you to know that. I'll never blame you for my brother. There's someone else who bears all the blame, he just doesn't know it.'

Outside, after the brightness of the morning, the sky had clouded over, bringing with it the threat of more rain. A chill wind had sprung up, and the fire that Hollinger had lit in the stove, to cook their meagre meal, was burning low. The stables were getting cold, but Hollinger could feel the heat from Cord's body as she sat close beside him. He was trying to hide just how distracting that was, but Cord wasn't fooled.

She gave him a knowing look as she said, 'It's got a mite chilly in here, don't you think?' When the marshal replied with a grunt she added, 'We'd be a lot warmer under this blanket than sitting on top of it.'

Hollinger did his best to look shocked. 'Cordelia Thornton! That is not the behaviour of a well-brought-up young lady.'

Cord grinned. There was a mischievous spark in her eyes as she leaned closer to him. 'But marshal dear, you know I wasn't well brought up, so if I was you I'd just take advantage of it.'

Before Hollinger knew what she intended, she'd thrown her arms around him and her lips were pressing against his own. He resisted for only a second, before wrapping his arms around her and pulling her close. The softness of her body, and the feminine scent of her drove all other thoughts from his mind.

'At long last,' Cord whispered breathlessly, as they sank back on to the narrow bunk.

There was a loud rending crack from beneath them. They jumped up, startled. The bunk was doing a slow collapse. Cord and the marshal looked at the bunk, then at each other, and then they laughed. They laughed until their sides were hurting, and while they laughed they forgot about what was to come.

When they pulled out later that day, they left three graves behind. Three mounds of dirt with a few stones piled up on top. That was all that marked the passing of Jinks Screeby, Riley Alvarez and Pardos Leghan. Hollinger prayed that there would be no more.

He prayed especially for the young woman who rode by his side.

CHAPTER NINE

SALLY AND THE SHOOTIST

In the Remuda saloon Miles Bracken and Leila Wendel stood on either side of the bar, leaning towards each other, their heads close. To a casual observer they looked like old friends, entirely at ease with each other, just sharing a drink and chewing the fat, perhaps discussing the town's business, and its scandals. But closer inspection would have shown that their attention was mutually focused on a man who sat alone near the back of the saloon. A dandy in a pearl grey frock-coat, whose hands never strayed too far from the ivory-handled pistols stuck in a red sash at his waist.

'What's he waiting for?' Leila complained. 'He's got to be here for the bounty, and yet he just sits. It's like he thinks the marshal is going to come to him. Just walk in here and allow that peacock to gun him down.' She knocked back the last of her drink. 'He's setting my nerves on edge, just seeing him so easy and relaxed.'

Bracken looked from Saul Quist to the empty tumbler. He'd never known Leila to drink her own whiskey. She had a rule about selling the stuff, but not consuming it. Not in public anyway. It showed how nervous she was that this evening was an exception. It was hardly surprising, seeing as how the entire town was on edge.

'He's not all that relaxed,' Bracken corrected her. 'Far from it. He tries to give that impression, but he's watching everything. He's wound so tight I keep expecting to hear him squeak.'

'But why's he just sitting there? Everyone else lit out after Ben yesterday.'

Quist had taken a room at the hotel, but he seemed to spend most of his time either sitting outside the establishment, from where he could watch the marshal's office, or in the saloon. Talk about him was all over town. Everyone knew why he was in Bannack, but his lack of action was a source of much speculation.

A card game was under way in the centre of the

room. As Sally Devon drifted past with a tray full of drinks for the players, Leila said, 'Sally, go light the lamps, will you. It's getting dark in here, and I want to keep an eye on that gentleman.' Dan Backus usually lit the lamps in the evening, but he was on guard duty with Jake Fallon over at the jail. Leila watched Sally deliver the drinks and then start on the lamps. Her movements were slow and uncoordinated, her expression vacant.

'She's not at all herself,' Leila said.

Bracken nodded sympathetically. Before Leto's death Sally's lively, fun-loving ways had endeared her to the saloon's many patrons. A redhead with a heart-shaped face and full lips that always seemed widened in a sunny smile, her enthusiasm and energy, and her infectious laughter, had been noted by all who frequented the Remuda. Now, she looked as though she could barely manage to get across the floor without falling over. But as she finished with the lamps Bracken was surprised, and a bit alarmed, to see her approach Saul Quist.

When she spoke her voice carried clear across the saloon. It sounded brittle and reckless. 'You been sitting there for two days, mister. We all would sure like to know what in hell you're waiting around for.'

Leila started around the counter, but Bracken caught her arm. He shook his head. Saul Quist wasn't likely to do Sally any harm. He was hunting much bigger game than a grief-stricken bar girl.

Quist narrowed his eyes as he looked up into Sally's face, his expression one of amused puzzlement. With a studied detachment he stroked the point of his beard, as though considering her question.

Deciding at last on an appropriate response, he said, 'Well, since you're such a pretty little thing, and you've asked me all polite, I'll tell you what I'm waiting for. I'm waiting to kill a man called Ben Hollinger who, according to general gossip, made the mistake of shooting a very rich man's only son. I hear tell that he's a scoundrel of the first order, and it'll be my pleasure to put him in the ground, just so he can't murder any more helpless children.'

'Billy Thornton weren't no child,' Sally said, her voice filled with bitterness. 'He was fixing to kill the man I loved. Marshal Hollinger is a good man, and them as says different is worthless, low-down scum.'

Quist cocked his head on one side, regarding Sally with dark amusement. 'You know, that sounded a lot like you were including me in that description. But I know that you couldn't possibly be that foolish. It would be both very rude and very dangerous.'

For a moment Sally just stood there, her eyes blank and her face wiped clean of expression. Then she leaned forward and spat right into Quist's face. 'I reckon that might tell you just what I think of you,' she said. Despite her actions her voice was still stripped of emotion.

Quist leapt up, his face twisted with fury. His arm swept back, but before he could deliver the blow he clearly intended, Leila had her arms around Sally and was pulling her away. Bracken stepped in front of the shootist. He said, 'You don't want to be doing that, mister.'

Quist glared at him, his colour high and his eyes flashing dangerously. 'And who's good enough to stop me?'

Bracken backed off, smiling gently. 'I don't reckon any of us need to stop you. You didn't come here to hurt nor kill no saloon girls. You do that and you can forget about the marshal. Your guns wouldn't stop you being run out of town.' Quist hesitated and Bracken added, 'Anger can't be that useful an emotion in your line of work, I should think. It could make you darn careless at just the wrong moment. Maybe get you killed.'

As the doctor spoke, Quist seemed to get control of himself. He took a deep breath and the colour faded from his cheeks. He sat back down, regarding Bracken with the same lazy amusement he'd first shown Sally. 'I don't get angry that often. But when I do, someone gets dead.'

'Maybe next time it'll be you,' Bracken said, before walking back to the bar.

The floodgates of grief had finally burst wide open, and Sally was crying bitterly into Leila's shoulder. 'Better get her out of here,' Bracken said. 'I wouldn't like to trust in that man's self control a second time tonight.'

As Leila hustled Sally away the doctor went back to watching Quist. He was more concerned than ever about what might happen when Ben Hollinger returned.

Hollinger waited inside the tree-line until he saw Cord coming with the wagon, her pinto tied to the rear. She had left his own dapple-grey with O'Rourke. He stepped out to greet her, figuring he was safe enough, despite Cord's understandable caution. A betting man would probably put money on him riding as far and as fast as possible, not heading back towards a town full of men who were eager to put a slug in him.

'Get in amongst the sacks and boxes,' Cord told him. 'Get well hid, and don't make no sound once we get close to the ranch. Ever since this started there have been guard patrols roaming all over the place. My father thought you might come after him, if no one shot you first.'

Hollinger settled down amongst a pile of flour sacks. As Cord slapped the reins and the wagon lurched into motion, he began checking his Colt and his Winchester. He'd brought Riley Alvarez's hunting rifle with him, plus the Mexican's ammunition belt, which was hung over his sheepskin coat. Very soon they left the riverside trail and skirted the town. Hollinger could feel Cord's tension at being so close to Bannack, but they passed without incident. Then they were moving into more open territory, joining the road that, a few miles further on, forked towards the Tumbling T ranch.

Towards dusk, as the wagon at last bumped and rattled its way on to Thornton land Cord leaned back towards him and said, 'Look at the sky.'

There was a blustery breeze, but few clouds moved in the vastness above them. There was a full moon rising. Very soon it would bathe the open range in a cold hard light.

'That moon won't be exactly helpful. Not when you're planning a stealthy night raid,' Cord said uneasily. 'It was cloudy most of the day. I hoped it would last. This is not good.'

'I reckon not,' Hollinger agreed. 'But I got no choice. You do, Cord, and I'd be happier if you bailed out about now. I'll go on in myself. No one's expecting me, so I got a more than even chance.'

'You weren't listening, Ben. I told you, my father expects you to make a move against him, sooner or later. I'm with you right down the line, so get used to it, partner.' She looked at the sky again, and chuckled.

'What are you finding that's amusing in all of this?' Ben asked.

'Something I been dreaming about for a long time. A wagon ride with Ben Hollinger, under the autumn moon. Don't you know how romantic this is?'

'Romantic?' Hollinger laughed. 'We're heading for a possible gunfight and you think it's romantic. Cord Thornton, you are the craziest gal I ever did come across.'

Although he couldn't see her up in the driver's seat, he could sense her looking back. 'Sure I'm crazy. You wouldn't love me if I wasn't.'

'Love you?' he spluttered. 'I never said—'

'Well, if that bunk hadn't broke on us you were going to love me real good.'

'Cord, you know that's not a proper way for a lady to talk.'

'And you know full well that I'm no lady, Ben. No good and proper lady would be standing by you with a gun in her hand, and that's what I'll be doing before this night is through. So you get your thinking right on this. When all this is over, and if we're both not shot full of holes, I'm coming after you, Ben Hollinger, and I intend to have you for my own. Now, you got anything to say to that?'

Hollinger thought about it for a moment. 'You're a lot more frightening than any bounty hunter, you know that?'

101

She said nothing more, but he could hear her giggling quietly to herself and he felt a surge of affection. Cordelia Thornton was one of a kind and no mistake. The man who claimed her, or whom she claimed, could count himself blessed. But even as he thought of spending the rest of his life with her, the past reared up before him. He saw dead and broken bodies littering his back trail, and more would be joining them very soon.

Cordelia deserved a lot better.

'We got company!' Cord hissed. A moment later he heard riders thundering down on them. Quite a few riders, from the sound of it.

As he pulled the flour sacks up over himself, and eased the hammer on his Colt to half-cock, he wondered if this was as far as he was going to get.

CHAPTER TEN

THE TUMBLING T

Cord reined in as the riders closed with her. There looked to be about a dozen of them. They were Tumbling T hands, well known to her, and yet they seemed almost sinister in the gathering twilight, their wide-brimmed hats and long slickers making them all look alike. At least three of them had rifles pointed towards her.

They had the wagon surrounded before the one in front recognized her. 'Miss Cordelia?'

'Wade Garrett, is that you?' She felt relieved. Wade was the one ranch hand she might be able to bluff. The two of them had hunted grouse together, gone fishing together, and done their share of cutting loose and raising hell whenever they hit town.

He was fresh-faced and fair-haired, and there had been a time when she'd looked favourably on Wade Garrett as a possible suitor, although her father would have raised the roof if he'd known. His displeasure wouldn't have stopped her, if anything it would have made her more determined, but then Wade had got himself a sweetheart in town, and she'd taken a liking to the new marshal.

'It's me, sure enough,' Wade replied. 'Why are you out here all alone? Your daddy wants the ranch locked up tight, until this business with the marshal is all settled.'

'Settled? You mean until Ben Hollinger is dead.'

Garrett shifted uneasily on his mount. 'I reckon so.'

'And you go along with that?'

Garrett shrugged. 'I don't see that I got much choice, Missy. Your daddy pays my wages, the same as every other man here.' He looked around for support.

A gravelly voice from behind Wade said, 'I go along with whatever Mr Thornton wants done, and so should you, being his daughter and all.' Cord recognized Ed Harker, an unpleasant man with mean eyes, whom she'd never taken to.

His opinion didn't seem to be too widely shared. Most of the men circling the wagon seemed as uneasy as Wade. He ran his gaze over the wagon and said, 'Anyways, Missy, what you got back there?'

'The usual. Flour, grain, coffee beans and such. Some bolts of cloth. What with the trouble in town the other day, we came away without some of the supplies I had on the list.'

'The trouble in town?' Harker barked. 'I guess you're talking about the way that law-dog murdered your brother right in front of your eyes.'

Cord bristled at his tone, but this was hardly the moment to challenge his description of events. Dislike between her and Harker was mutual, and if anyone was likely to be suspicious of her it was him. He was another one of Billy's friends, and he knew how much Billy had disapproved of her feelings towards Ben Hollinger. The last thing she wanted was Harker thinking how close she and the marshal might be.

'I do know what happened, Harker,' she told him. 'Do you think I'll ever forget seeing my own brother gunned down?'

Harker grimaced, his outrage slightly appeased by her tone. 'I reckon not. You got as much reason to hate Hollinger as anyone. The boss reckons that fool doctor and others might get a posse riding out here, maybe with Hollinger leading them. If they do, they're gonna ride right into hell.'

Behind her, Cord was aware of one of the cowboys leaning over for a better look at the wagon's contents. 'Well, I better get on up to the house,' she said.

'Two of us will ride in with you,' Wade said. 'Stoner, you come with me. The rest of you keep watch for any unexpected visitors.' Stoner, a quiet man with broad shoulders and thick limbs, nodded and urged his mount alongside the wagon.

'That isn't necessary,' Cord protested. 'I can take the wagon in myself.'

Wade shook his head. 'The boss won't like you being out here all alone. I'm guessing he don't know you went into town all by yourself, so we'll be keeping you company, Missy, until you're safe home.'

Further argument would likely cause suspicion, so Cord just slapped the reins and got the horses moving. As the wagon headed in, it was flanked by Wade and Stoner. Concealed in the back Ben Hollinger had heard every word of the exchange. What was he going to do if the two cowhands helped unload the wagon? He knew Wade and Stoner to be decent men. He couldn't just shoot them to get to Nate Thornton. He could only hope that Cord might persuade them against helping with the unloading.

The forty acres that held the ranch house, with all its corrals and outbuildings, was entered by a wide iron gate that had the sideways-leaning capital T worked into the archway. It sat right on the summit of a slight rise. As the wagon passed under it, and the ranch buildings spread out beneath her, Cord felt her tension increase. She wasn't alone in feeling that way. Ranch hands were wandering about armed to the teeth, clearly expecting trouble. It was a tension you could cut through, and not just because a posse might come storming in at any moment. Many of the men were deeply unhappy with the situation.

With a few exceptions, most of them were basically law-abiding. They might do a little hell-raising now and then, but there was no real harm intended. They were being asked to set themselves against the law, and it didn't sit right with many.

Cord saw this confusion on many faces, but not all. There were those few who had backed Billy in whatever dishonest and violent play he made, and who had grudges against the marshal. And then there was the lure of money, which was temptation enough for some men to kill.

She took the wagon around to the back of the house. The two-storey frame structure had rooms on either side of a central hallway that was roofed over, with rooms above, but which was open to the world at either end. Wide verandas ran along two sides of the house. Cord pulled up by the last room on the north side, a storeroom that led into a large kitchen.

Her intention had been for Ben to slip inside the

storeroom, but as Stoner dismounted and dropped the tailgate, Wade told him to help her unload. At least Wade wasn't waiting around. He said he better get back to the others and he galloped off.

Stoner heaved a sack off the wagon, and Cord said, 'I'll do that. I know where everything needs to go. You tell my father I'm back. He might have been worrying about me.'

'Sure,' Stoner said. 'I'll just get the heavier stuff moved first.' He carried his burden inside, then came back out and started lifting another sack, before something caught his attention. He stared into the wagon for a second, dropped the sack and went for his gun. Cord, coming round behind him, saw the heel of the marshal's boot giving away his presence.

Without thinking she grabbed Stoner's hand, preventing him from pulling the gun from its holster. Surprised by her sudden action, he shouted something unintelligible and tried to shake her off. She was Thornton's daughter, and that stopped him from dealing with her too violently, but he was a lot stronger than Cord. He was close to freeing his gun hand when Hollinger flung the flour sacks aside and saw what was happening.

Stoner pushed Cord aside and got his gun out. Hollinger was still off balance in the wagon. It was clear that Stoner had him. Cord didn't think he'd shoot, but he would have the marshal covered while he called for help. Cord drew back her arm and let fly. Her closed fist hit Stoner hard on the side of his nose. There was a sickening crack and Stoner cried out. So did Cord, as a shock of pain jolted her hand and wrist.

Stoner grabbed for his injured nose, and Cord seized his gun hand once again, this time with her uninjured hand, pulling its aim away from the marshal. By that time Hollinger was on him. He jumped from the wagon, taking Stoner down with him. As they hit the dirt, with Stoner underneath, Hollinger hit him on the jaw. Stoner blinked away the blow and tried to heave the marshal off. He was a strong man and he wasn't going to go down easy. He was also about to call for help.

There was dull thud, and Stoner's eyes rolled up in his head. He slumped back on the ground, unconscious. Hollinger looked up to see Cord holding the pistol she'd managed to wrestle away from the cowhand. She'd clubbed him over the head with it. Stoner was out cold.

'I'm truly sorry,' she half-whispered in the man's ear. She glanced at the marshal. 'It had to be done.'

Hollinger looked at her, standing there rubbing at her hand and wrist, with her honey-coloured hair all messed up and the colour high in her cheeks. Her green eyes had an almost feral look to them. He

shook his head in disbelief. 'You never fail to surprise me,' he said.

She tried to flex her fingers. 'That really hurt!'
The hand that had struck Stoner was already starting
to bruise quite badly. 'We better get him well hid.
You think he'll be out for long?'

'Long enough,' Hollinger said. It took some effort
to heave the burly cowhand up on to his shoulder.
Cord opened the storeroom door and he staggered
inside, easing his burden down behind a stack of
boxes. 'Which way?' he said.

'Through that door, then on through the
kitchen.'

The kitchen was empty. With Cord leading, they
moved from the kitchen out into the open hallway.
Voices came from the middle door on the opposite,
south-facing side. One of the voices belonged to
Nate Thornton.

Thornton was pacing about the room, a whiskey
glass in his hand, agitation showing in his restless
movement. His face was red from the whiskey. In the
room with him were Sam Mooney and Hamilton
Bell. Mooney was his reserved, watchful self, sucking
on his unlit pipe, but Bell was white-faced and clearly
panicked. Mooney was seated, but Bell was standing,
near rigid with fear, pleading with his client.

'I tell you, Nate, the town won't stand for any

110

more of it. That bounty has turned the streets into a bloodbath.'

Thornton gave him a contemptuous look. 'What is it, Hamilton? Are you afraid for your professional standing?'

Bell flinched under his client's stare. 'If this gets any worse I'm finished in Bannack, that's sure enough. But I'm more concerned about the effect this will have on you, Nate.'

Thornton's lip curled. 'Of course you are. I'd never think otherwise. I'd never accuse you of being a spineless snivelling toad with water between your legs. No, I'd never believe that.'

Bell wasn't sure how to take Thornton's words. He stammered, 'Listen, Nate, it's not too late to stop this thing.'

'That's right.' Mooney had been silent up to now, but his tone was scathing as he spoke to Bell. 'You could just go into town and tell the crowd of killers gathering there that there's no money, and they came all that way for nothing. Since you were the one put the word out, I think you're the one to put a stop to it. I'm sure that bunch of murderous cut-throats will take it real well.'

Thornton turned bloodshot eyes on Mooney, his mouth turned down in displeasure. 'You've been against this from the start, Sam. I would have expected more loyalty from you.'

Mooney shook his head. 'Loyalty is all that's kept me here these last couple of days, because you're wrong about this, Mr Thornton, dead wrong. Billy went—'

'I won't hear a word against my son!' Thornton snarled. He threw his whiskey glass into the fireplace. The glass shattered and the flames flared up briefly, casting his face in a demonic glow. 'That damned lawman murdered him, and he's going to pay for it. He's going straight to hell!'

'But you're going first!' Hollinger said from the doorway.

CHAPTER ELEVEN

'NO ONE GETS OUT OF HERE ALIVE'

Stepping into the room, the marshal covered the three men with his Winchester.

'Hollinger? How did you—?' As Cord followed the marshal in, carrying the hunting rifle Hollinger had taken from Riley Alvarez, there was both shock and bitter disappointment on her father's face. 'You brought him here? You did this? My own daughter?'

Cord didn't answer. Instead she went over to the window and peered out on to the veranda. Seeing no one, she pulled the heavy velvet curtains over. Only then did she look her father straight in the eye. Her chin lifted defiantly. 'I brought him here. I've been in town, and I've seen what this madness has brought to the people there. A young mother is dead, shot down by one of your men, one of Billy's mad-dog friends. It has to stop, father.'

Thornton pointed a finger at the marshal, his hand trembling with rage. 'That man murdered your brother, and you take his side, you bring him here?'

'The marshal didn't murder nobody.'

'Your brother—'

'Billy was no good. I always knew that. I guess I loved him some because he was my brother, but he was mean and cruel and vicious, and I guess he got that from you. I did some hell-raising myself, but nothing like what Billy did. I never meant no harm to anyone, but Billy, he just enjoyed the hell out of hurting folks. I don't think you ever knew the half of it. I heard stories that chilled me to the bone.'

'Pah! Stories! Tall tales told when him and his friends were drunk and shooting their mouths off.'

'No, father, it wasn't just tall tales. Billy was already a killer before he started the fight in the saloon. He just ran out of luck when he tried to shoot the marshal.'

'If Billy killed anyone it was most likely because they asked for it. Some people just need killing.'

Cord stared at him as though seeing him for the first time, then she slowly shook her head. 'I guess that's how you think, isn't it? I heard stories about you as well. About how you grabbed this land, and how you held on to it. How much blood is on your hands, father? How much of your pure meanness did you pass on to Billy? I guess you're more responsible for killing my brother than Ben is.'

Thornton looked as though he was about to strike her, but Hollinger stepped in between them. The old man's eyes were blazing with anger. 'You're no daughter of mine. I don't ever want to see you again. You set foot on this ranch and—'

'And what? What will you do, father? Have me shot for trespassing?'

'That's enough, Cord,' Hollinger said gently. He aimed the rifle at Thornton. 'I'm taking you in for threatening the life of a peace officer, and for causing the unlawful deaths of Leto Picken and Sasha Barlow.' He looked over at Hamilton Bell, who had been standing to one side, silent and fearful, since the marshal entered the room. 'I think you should advise your client not to resist.'

Sam Mooney had remained seated throughout the exchange. His uneasy gaze had flitted from Hollinger to Cord to Thornton, and he seemed to be listening for sounds beyond the room. Now he said, 'Marshal, how in hell do you plan on getting him past a ranch full of armed men?'

Thornton gave a twisted grin at his foreman's

words. 'He can't. Trying to get me out of here is plain suicide. Out here, on my land, I'm the only law that counts. You'll be cut down before you get a dozen paces.'

'Maybe, but you'll be cut down right along with me,' Hollinger replied, iron in his voice and in his eyes. 'Whatever happens, Thornton, you'll be the first to die. I'll make sure of that. What about you, Mooney? I always had you pegged as somebody with more sense than most. Are you going to set yourself against the law?'

'You got some grit in you, marshal, I'll give you that. But I don't rightly know what to do here.'

Cord said, 'You do what's right, Sam Mooney.'

Mooney lowered his head, tucking the unlit pipe back into his shirt pocket. As he raised his eyes again, he looked beyond the marshal and shouted, 'Behind you!'

Hollinger leapt aside as a meat cleaver sliced the air where his head had been. He swung the rifle in a short arc, and Thornton's cook took the blow across his forehead. He crashed to the ground, but a frightened face was glimpsed in the doorway. A moment later someone was running along the hallway.

'Well, I guess that's about torn it,' Mooney said. 'Whoever that was they'll raise the alarm for sure.'

Hollinger pointed towards a gun cabinet in the far corner. 'Mr Bell,' he snapped, 'fetch me one of

116

those Greeners out of the cabinet, and a box of shells.'

The lawyer was shaking, his face white and sweating. He flapped his hands in panic. 'No! No, no, no! I'll have nothing to do with this. I'm leaving here right now, you hear me. You let me out of here! This is none of my concern!'

Hollinger swung the rifle towards him. There was commotion outside the window, and he heard men approaching down the hallway. 'I heard Mooney saying how you spread word of the bounty, so I hold you as much to blame as your client in all of this. If I was you I wouldn't be pressing my luck.'

Bell looked too frightened to move, but Cord leaned the hunting rifle against the wall by the window and swept past him. She opened the gun cabinet, loaded a shotgun and passed it to the marshal, who handed her his Winchester.

'You don't have to do this,' Hollinger said. 'He is your father, Cord.'

'I'm doing it,' Cord said grimly. 'Accept it.'

Hollinger nodded, his expression both fearful and admiring. He pulled Thornton over facing the door, then placed himself directly behind the rancher.

The first one to peer through the doorway was a ranch hand called Davis, but there were others crowded behind him in the hallway. He saw

Thornton standing with his hands at his side, and the marshal standing directly behind him.

'Boss?' he said.

'I got a shotgun stuck in his back,' Hollinger told him. 'Anybody trying to get in here will be responsible for it going off. You tell the others to stay out. Tell a couple of those boys behind you to drag the cook out of here.' While they did as the marshal said, Davis shot quick glances around the room, at Hollinger and his boss, at Cord and Bell, and Mooney still sat in the chair, then he backed out.

'Bell, you close that door,' Hollinger ordered. 'Shove some furniture in front of it.'

While the still shaking lawyer did as he was told, the marshal instructed Thornton to sit in the other armchair, on the far side of the fireplace from Mooney. There was a small table beside the chair, with a whiskey decanter and a glass sitting on it. Almost casually, as though he were relaxing for the evening, Thornton settled back and poured himself a drink.

Cord went over to the door, listened, and then shoved a small ornamental table more securely into the barricade that the lawyer had made. Hamilton Bell moved away from her, his eyes jumping nervously between Cord and the marshal. 'We need to close off that other door as well,' Cord told him. 'It's my father's study. They could come through the window in there.'

While they were doing that, Hollinger nodded his thanks to Mooney. 'You saved me from getting my head split. I owe you.'

'You'll pay for your treachery, Sam Mooney,' Thornton growled.

Mooney had clearly had enough. He turned on his employer with anger flaring in his eyes. 'Give it up, Mr Thornton! It's finished! Either the marshal is going to take you in, or both of you are going to die in the attempt, but whichever way it goes, you're done.'

'You think so?' Thornton sneered. 'Better men than you and Hollinger have crossed me up. Pretty soon you'll both be joining them under the dirt.'

Hollinger called out to the men in the hallway. 'You hear me out there? I got a shotgun on your boss. I'm coming out in a few minutes, with the Greener stuck in his back. If you don't have a wagon waiting for me, or if anyone tries anything at all, I'll pull the trigger. You'll get me, but your boss will have to be picked up with a shovel.'

Thornton surged up out of his chair, yelling, 'If he comes out you kill him! Kill them all! No one gets out of here alive!'

Hollinger drove the stock of the shotgun into his stomach. Thornton gasped in pain and fell back into the chair. Fighting for breath he glared up at the marshal, hate and fury in his eyes.

'You really are a crazy old man,' Hollinger said mildly.

The lamps in the room had been extinguished, and the fire was burning low. For the last twenty minutes or so there had been little movement from the hallway, just an occasional scuffling and whispering.

'This is a pretty desperate play you're making,' Mooney told the marshal.

'Desperate and foolish,' Hamilton Bell added. 'If you'll allow me, Marshal, I can go out and talk to Davis and the others. Perhaps we can settle this without violence. If they agree to let you leave unharmed, alone and without Mr Thornton, perhaps we can deal with the legal matters once you're safely back in town. If the bounty is lifted—'

'When hell freezes over!' Thornton snapped.

I know about hell, Hollinger thought. I've been there.

Even now, so many years later, in the still of the night, he heard the dying screams of his mother as the bullets hit her, again and again, dull slapping sounds that twisted and jerked her body around until it finally hit the ground and moved no more. The hatred that had burned in him had been brighter and hotter than all the flames of hell. In his nightmares he still saw the faces of the men he had hunted, the light dying from their eyes as he killed them, one by one, after walking into fights of such viciousness and brutality that most men would hesitate and think of their own safety. He'd had no fear in him, the hatred in his soul had seen to that. Hate twisted you so much that normal concerns just disappeared from your thinking.

Was it that same hatred, that he'd known for so long, that Nate Thornton felt for him? Where they really that different? He'd killed to avenge his family, and Thornton wanted vengeance for his son. He could understand that.

Why hadn't he just left town, gone to seek help, or maybe dropped his badge on the desk and ridden out? So many had died in the last few days, and he'd slaughtered most of them. How many more would he take with him, and why? Was it really to uphold the law, or did some dark and secret part of him want this? His skill in the taking of human life had come back to him far too easily.

He felt Cord's hand on his. There was a gentle understanding in her gaze, as though she knew what troubled him. 'You didn't bring this on us,' she whispered. 'It wasn't anything you did, it was Billy and my father. They started this. They gave you no chance at all to do it different.'

It was as though she'd read his mind, seen the fear in him of what he might be, the killer hidden inside who still craved the death of others. He squeezed her hand, but didn't answer.

'Doc says that you were a rancher once.'

'A long time ago.'

'It can't be that long. You're still young.'

'Hell no, Cord, I ain't been young since. . . .'

'Since you watched your family killed by outlaws on the dodge.'

'Doc talks too much.'

'He has to, since you don't talk at all. Pain doesn't have to be endured all by yourself, you know.' There was such a sweetness in her deep, green eyes that Hollinger was forced to turn away. 'You think I'm too good for you, Ben Hollinger, is that it? It's the very opposite that's true. I'm spoilt, opinionated and entirely too wayward for my own good. I was almost as rotten as my brother when I was growing up. But I'm all grown up now, and I'm not my brother or my father. I'm trying to be a better person, a responsible citizen, someone decent who might someday be worthy of Ben Hollinger's love and respect.'

'I'm not the man you think I am.'

She put a hand to his face and turned it towards her own. 'Yes you are. You're exactly the man I think you are.' Leaning in, she kissed him with a loving gentleness.

Sitting across from them, Nate Thornton's eyes glittered with hate.

CHAPTER TWELVE

UNDER SIEGE

'Well, looky here!' Thornton spat. 'Ain't that just dandy! Kissing the man who murdered your brother. You got no shame, have you, girl? You two sure have had a lot to say to each other. Seeing as how you hanker after each other so much, I'll see you get buried together.'

Cord dropped her head, too ashamed to meet her father's gaze. But it wasn't shame over kissing the marshal, it was shame that this man – this ruthless, cruel, insane old man – was her father. She thought of Billy, who had never been the sharpest mind around, and she thought: he never had a chance. He had been infected from birth with his father's callous disregard for anything but his own needs.

'The thing I'll never understand,' Hollinger was saying to Thornton, 'is how you ever had a daughter as fine as Cordelia. I never knew her mother, but I have to assume she takes after her, because she sure don't take after you.'

'I reckon you're right about that.' Thornton shot a look of disgust towards his daughter. 'She's just like her mother was, weak and disloyal. The only mistake I ever made was marrying spineless Eastern society trash, all lace and no grit.'

Cord stared at him, pale and shaken by his words, but her voice was firm and determined when she spoke. 'You call Ben a murderer, but you as good as murdered your own wife. I always wondered about that accident, about why my mother was out there alone, and why she would be crossing the Snake when it was riding high. I heard what you said to Sam, about how she killed herself. I guess she couldn't live with your cruelty any more. I guess I can't live with it either, but I don't figure on killing myself. I've got another way to be rid of you.' She aimed the Winchester at his head. 'If the marshal don't get you with that Greener, you still got me to worry about.'

Thornton sneered. 'You'll be sharing a grave with your marshal before this night is over.'

Hollinger stared at the man as if he was seeing a rattlesnake getting too close. 'You'd have your own daughter killed? What kind of a man are you, Thornton?'

'One who's danced on the graves of everyone who ever got in my way.'

Hollinger looked into the hate-filled eyes. 'I don't doubt it. I think it's way past your time for dying, old man, and no matter what happens next, I intend to see it gets done. If your men try to stop me you'll get this shotgun's full load. Then the gun hands among your crew, and the bounty hunters in town, won't have no more stake in proceedings, because there'll be no one to pay them for their efforts. They might get me, but they won't have no cause to do harm to anyone else.'

The fury on Thornton's face was thin reward, but it still cheered the marshal some. He knew the old man was right; his chances of getting off the ranch with his prisoner were slim. All he could do was try to keep Cord and Sam Mooney alive. But could he kill Nate Thornton in cold blood? He'd killed so many times before, with the same ice-cold determination that he needed now. Was he the same man, the same killer of men that he'd been for so many years. He'd prayed that he wasn't, that the man he'd been was gone for good, and yet now he needed to be that man again, if Cord and Mooney were to live.

There was a shout from the hallway. 'The wagon's all ready for you.'

'Pull everyone back, away from the house,' Hollinger shouted back. He looked at Hamilton Bell, who was in no danger from the men outside. 'Clear the doorway,' he ordered.

Once the door was cleared of the piled-up furniture, Hollinger shouted, 'We're coming out! Any shooting you'll likely hit your boss!' He turned to Mooney and asked how many he thought there might be, waiting out there in the gathering darkness.

'I reckon maybe no more than a dozen or so, probably led by Davis. He'll follow Thornton's orders, and that bounty will surely be of interest to him. The rest will sit it out, not sure what they should be doing.'

'Any man that don't back me is fired!' Thornton growled.

Hollinger stared at him, shaking his head in mock sorrow. 'You really are about two-thirds of the way crazy, and that last third is going fast. You still don't appreciate how you'll be way too dead to be firing anyone.'

Telling Hamilton Bell to walk in front of them, Hollinger urged his prisoner out of the door. Seeing that Cord and Mooney were about to follow he said, 'You both stay here. I don't need you, and the fewer targets the better.'

Mooney drew his pistol. 'I just quit Mr Thornton's

employ, so I'm with you, like it or not. You'll need an extra pair of eyes out there.'

Cord said, 'Don't think about trying to stop me, Ben.' Her jaw was set, and Hollinger knew she meant it.

The open-ended hallway was empty. A strengthening wind blew along the length of it, coming in from the west. The tense little procession turned the other way, heading towards the wagon they could see waiting just beyond the last two rooms on the eastern side. As they stepped out into the open, the moon threw their shadows along the ground.

'Drop the tailgate,' Hollinger told Hamilton Bell. He kept the Greener pushed up hard against his prisoner's back. Mooney swept the area with his pistol, Cord with her rifle. There was no one in sight. There were undoubtedly guns out there, aimed in their direction, but well hidden in the many outbuildings. The only lamps lit were in the furthest bunkhouse, well away from all the trouble. That was where the ranch hands who were sitting it out were probably gathered, arguing amongst themselves as to the proper course of action.

'Climb into the back of the wagon,' Hollinger told Bell. He shouted out to the watchers, 'I got this Greener jammed in Thornton's spine, so if anyone gets all jittery and trigger-happy, your boss will be in hell one second before me.'

Hamilton Bell stumbled as he tried to climb into the wagon, fell backwards a step into Thornton and the marshal. Thornton seized him by the shoulders and flung him round, shoving him hard. He stumbled into Hollinger, knocking the shotgun aside. Thornton was running before Hollinger could get clear of the lawyer. Mooney snapped off a shot, but it went wide.

The second Thornton was clear, the shooting began. Hamilton Bell, still standing in front of the marshal, took the first volley of shots. Bullets peppered his upper torso and face, slamming him backwards once more into the marshal. A scream died in his throat, replaced by a retching gurgle as blood poured out of his mouth.

'Back in the house!' Hollinger yelled.

Cord and Mooney ran back into the open hallway. The shooting was concentrated on the marshal, who staggered backwards, heading for cover with both arms around the dying lawyer. Bullets kept hitting Bell, making him jump and shudder in the marshal's embrace. Once inside the hallway, Hollinger laid him down. His lips were speckled with blood-flecked foam, his eyes showing disbelief and terror at the manner of his own violent death. As a continuous hail of lead hammered the walls and hallway, Bell's eyes finally glazed over.

'Don't be grieving for him, marshal,' Mooney

said. 'He could have told Thornton to go to hell when he was asked to put out word of the bounty. He's as guilty as Thornton is. I reckon we all are. All of us who stood by and did nothing to stop this.'

Cord was staring at the lawyer's body, pity and horror mixed in her expression.

Running figures were closing in on the hallway, getting into position for a better shot along the darkened corridor. The hail of bullets didn't let up, becoming more accurate by the second.

'We better get back in the house,' Mooney said. 'Barricade ourselves in again. This is gonna be a siege, and there ain't no help coming. Thornton was the only advantage we had. Nothing will stop them now.'

The words had hardly left his lips when he convulsed in pain, and collapsed on top of the lawyer's body.

'Mooney!' Hollinger yelled.

'It's my leg!' Mooney gasped. 'Got me in the leg!'

Hollinger seized him under the armpits, hauling him towards the big room they had so recently vacated. Cord threw the door open and they staggered in, falling to the floor as the window shattered and gunfire ripped into the room, tearing the armchairs apart and pockmarking the walls. Hollinger helped her overturn the massive dining table, then they pulled Mooney behind it.

Sheltered behind the heavy wood, Cord looked at the foreman's blood-soaked leg. 'I think it went through the fatty part of the calf,' she told him.

'It hurts like hell! I can't walk, but I can still shoot. Give me the Greener, Marshal, and I'll see what damage I can do to the first one through that door.'

Out in the night they heard Nate Thornton's voice, filled with unholy triumph and shouting orders to go in and get them.

The first man who tried walked straight into a shotgun blast that knocked him back into the hallway. After that they became more cautious. Cord and Hollinger sent a few slugs through the shattered window by way of a warning. The men outside backed off a little, but Mooney was right, there was no help coming, and the three of them couldn't hold off Thornton's men for long.

Wade Garrett rose to his full height in the stirrups, watching anxiously as the rider approached. He'd heard shooting, a lot of it, coming from the direction of the ranch house.

Garrett's first thought had been of Cord. There had been something in her manner earlier that had disturbed him, a reserve that wasn't natural to her. The supply wagon was bothering him as well. Why would Cord, reckless as she was, take a foolish risk like going into Bannack alone, with all that had happened? Why would her father allow it? And what had happened to Stoner? He hadn't returned from helping her unload the wagon.

It was only after he'd returned to his patrol duty that such misgivings had started. He had been cursing himself for swallowing her story so easily. He'd got into enough scrapes with Cord in the past to know how impetuous she could be. He'd been on the verge of riding back to the ranch when the shooting started.

The lone rider began shouting before he was even up on the patrol. The wind snatched most of his words away. What Garrett heard seemed beyond belief.

'Cord?' he demanded, as the rider reined in alongside him. 'Cord is with the marshal?'

The rider was a young cowhand called Jacob Newby. He'd joined the outfit as a horse-wrangler during the summer. Care of the remuda was usually left to the youngest and least experienced of the men. Newby looked even more callow now, frightened and confused, and babbling out a story about the boss laying siege to the ranch house, with Cord and Ben Hollinger and Sam Mooney trapped inside.

'Most of the men are in one of the bunkhouses,' Newby said. 'They're staying out of it, but Davis and some others are backing the boss. They've been told to kill the marshal, and anyone who's helping him.'

Garrett understood the confusion that was staying the hand of most of the ranch workers. Most cowboys were loyal to their brand and their outfit, sometimes having to take arms against Indian attacks and rustler bands. But Nate Thornton had been stretching that loyalty for a long time with his ruthless ways. Garrett himself had chosen to turn a blind eye to certain goings-on. Such work had been taken on by Davis and Billy Thornton, with the help of some others on the ranch. Work like the disappearance of those free-grazers a while back, and running off their neighbour Svenson's cattle, and poisoning his well.

The bounty on the marshal's head had disturbed most of the men, and the killing of a young mother had set them to questioning their loyalty. Garrett remembered Cord's question of earlier in the evening. She'd asked if he went along with what her father was doing. He knew that he didn't. And now the old man had turned on his own daughter.

'Who sent you to get us?' Garrett asked.

'Nobody sent me,' Newby answered, his voice shaking with fear and desperation. 'I just couldn't stay there. I know you and Miss Cordelia are friends. You've got to help her, Wade. The boss has ordered the killing of everyone in the house. Miss Cordelia, she's in there as well.'

'Nobody's gonna hurt Missy!' Garrett said. He

turned to the others. 'I aim to stop this. Who'll ride with me?'

Harker, who had listened with a deepening scowl, reached for his gun. 'You ain't stopping nothing,' he snarled.

It was as far as he got. Another rider, called 'Turkey' Brookmeyer, clubbed him across the back of the head with his rifle butt. Harker fell from the saddle.

'Anyone else of the same opinion?' Turkey asked. He was the oldest of the Tumbling T hands, a white-haired, crusty old-timer with deep wrinkles and sagging jowls.

Garrett looked around him at the shocked faces. He said, 'I don't know what you all think about what's been happening in town, but I can't stomach no more young mothers being gunned down in the street, and the boss threatening to kill his own daughter. I don't work for him no more, but you all got to follow your own conscience. I'm riding in, and I'm planning on helping the marshal.'

Three decided they were riding with Garrett, the others were staying out of it. The three were Turkey, the scared but determined young horse-wrangler, and a cowboy called Tate.

'You'd best tie Harker down,' Turkey advised those who were remaining behind. 'He's got a mean temper at the best of times, and when he wakes he'll have one hell of a sore head.' He turned to Newby. 'You sure you want to do this, son?'

The boy looked frightened, but he replied in a firm enough tone, 'It's the right thing to do, I reckon.'

The four riders set off at a gallop. Their expressions grim and determined, Turkey, Tate and Newby rode alongside Garrett.

They were stopped at the iron gate by two men with rifles.

'What you want here, Wade?' one of the men called.

'That you, Crandell? I want to know what the shooting is all about, and why you're pointing that rifle at me?'

'We got us a situation here, but we're handling it. You can just clear on out.'

Garrett gave Turkey a look and saw that he understood. Taking his hat off and sounding confused, Garrett said, 'Nobody ever tells me anything. I guess I just never got the word that you'd been made foreman of this outfit.' As he spoke, he eased his cow pony sideways, partly blocking the view Crandell and his partner had of Turkey.

Crandell licked his lips nervously. He didn't like Garrett's mocking tone, and he had little confidence in his own position. He was there to stop anyone heading for the ranch, but he was far from happy about it. 'I don't want none of that smart talk,' he said. 'All of you just git! We'll tell you when to come back in.'

'All right, if that's the way you feel about it.' Garrett swung his pony away, leaving Crandell and his partner exposed to Turkey's rifle, which was aimed and spitting lead before either man could react.

Crandell went down, and his partner jumped back, trying to shoot as he went. A slug from Garrett's pistol spun him sideways before he dropped.

Up ahead the sound of gunfire was continuous. With Wade Garrett leading the charge, the four of them went storming into battle, guns blazing.

CHAPTER THIRTEEN

WADE'S
IRREGULARS

Darkness had fallen over Bannack, but there were still a great many people on the main street. Most of them were strangers to the town, and most of them were carrying guns as if they meant to use them.

Standing by the window in the marshal's office, Miles Bracken watched them drift up and down the street, the tension clear to see in their stiff, self-conscious movements, and in the wariness of their narrowed eyes as they swept the street from end to end, waiting for the moment when Ben Hollinger might show himself.

136

Dan Backus was sitting behind Hollinger's desk, enjoying a cup of coffee that was as black as tar, while Frank Orchin was taking an evening meal to the prisoner back in the cells. The drifter, Hollis, had given them no trouble since being locked up. The broken shoulder seemed to have taken all the fight out of him. Shooting at his intended victim from the shadows in a darkened street was one thing, taking on a group of armed men was another. It was clear that whatever courage he'd shown, it had been fuelled by drink and the lure of what he thought would be easy money.

Since the marshal rode out the town had been quiet. Local residents had tried to stay off the streets, for fear of more gunplay. Hollinger was gone, but the desperate-looking men who infested the town ensured that no one felt safe.

Jake Fallon pushed through the door after doing a solitary patrol. 'There's more of them by the hour,' he said.

'I don't like you going out there alone,' Bracken told him.

'There ain't no price on my head, Doc, I'm just the deputy.'

'But somebody might think to get a little practice in.'

Fallon laughed. 'You worry too much. You sound like my poor old momma. You sort of look like her too. She has some lip moss just like yours.'

'Thanks. I'll be sure and compare soon as I see her. I'm sure she'll be happy to hear what her son's been saying.' He looked out into the street again. 'You'd think what Ben did to that first bunch would have scared some of them off.'

Over behind the desk, Dan Backus snorted. 'That sort don't scare easy, not when there's a pile of money involved. They don't have the brains to be scared.'

'What about Quist?' Bracken asked.

'Still sitting there, waiting. The saloon's mighty quiet, not too many people wanting to be in there right now. Not among the locals anyway. The drifters are bad enough, but Quist has a way of spooking folk, the way he just sits. Like some vulture waiting for something to die.'

'He spooks everyone but Sally,' Bracken said.

'Yeah. Sally.' Fallon looked troubled. 'Leila says she won't stay in her room, and she's worried about what she might do, given her state of mind.'

As Frank Orchin came out from the cells, Bracken began to pace. His tone was anxious when he said, 'I wish we knew how it's working out for Ben.'

'I hope you were right about that girl,' Orchin said. 'When she took that wagon from me she was looking mighty grim and determined. Leila told me how she looked at Ben after he killed her brother. I been worrying it was the same look, one that don't bode well for the marshal. So I hope you're right to trust her, Doc.'

Bracken had been reflecting on this very same question, ever since he'd watched her leave town. 'I hope so too,' he said.

'If Jed Lowry got through there'll be a cavalry detachment here by tomorrow,' Backus reminded them. 'Once they ride in, all them drifters and gun hands will high-tail it out.'

His brow furrowed with worry, Bracken wondered whether Ben Hollinger would still be alive tomorrow.

For close on twenty minutes the room had been a black hell of noise and gunsmoke. Hollinger had extinguished the lamps before taking cover with Cord and Mooney, while a steady hail of lead had turned the once handsome room into a ruin. Expensive furniture was ripped apart, ornaments and lamps shattered, book pages fluttered around like dying birds, and the walls were pitted with bullet holes. The ivory white of the Axminster carpet was littered with wreckage, and spotted with blood from Mooney's leg wound.

'If I ain't dead after this is over,' Mooney had shouted, 'I'll sure enough be deaf.'

The steady hail of lead had petered out at last,

replaced by random shots designed to keep their heads down. Hollinger and Cord returned fire when they could, just to let their attackers know what they were risking if they came charging in, but they knew that their situation was hopeless. All Thornton had to do was wait. Sooner or later they'd run out of ammunition, then they wouldn't be able to stop any assault.

When all shooting eventually stopped, the silence that followed was even more threatening.

'They're getting ready to rush us,' Mooney said. 'They figure we're maybe out of bullets, and they got a lot more firepower anyway.' He slapped the thick expensive wood of Thornton's massive dining table. 'If it weren't for this, we'd be full of holes already. I reckon it'll take more than a brisk polishing to fix it up again.'

Hollinger heard the sound of another round being levered into Cord's Winchester. He could just about make out the soft pale blur of her face close beside him. She was ready to go out fighting, no doubt about that. He felt a surge of feeling for her, admiration mixed with pride and a love he'd denied admitting to himself for far too long.

'Let them come,' he heard her whisper. 'I just hope my father's leading the charge.'

As the silence dragged on, Mooney hissed, 'What are they waiting for?'

His question was answered a moment later by a soft whooshing noise. Hollinger ducked his head around the corner of the table for a quick look. The glow of leaping flames told him all he needed to know.

'They're getting ready to burn us out,' he said.

Mooney seemed to be listening to more than the rising crackle of flames. 'You hear riders coming in?' he asked.

Hollinger heard it too. The drumming of hoofs, getting louder by the second. 'You're right. Someone's coming, and they're coming fast.'

Outside, the sound of gunfire resumed, but it sounded like a lot more guns had joined in. For a moment Hollinger wondered whether reinforcements had arrived, whether maybe the ranch hands who'd been sitting it out had changed their minds once their boss was free. But not a single bullet seemed aimed at the house. Then they heard the screams of wounded or dying men.

Seeing that the marshal was about to move out from behind the table, Cord caught hold of his arm. 'What's happening? Where are you going?'

'Somebody's started a war out there. I mean somebody besides you and me. That's a lot of guns going off, and all of a sudden no one's shooting at us. I have to see what's happening.'

'What was that?' Mooney hissed. 'What did you

say? Who started a war?'

'You and Cord stay here,' Hollinger told him.

As he crabbed across the floor he heard someone running outside, along the veranda. He raised his Colt, ready to shoot, but didn't need to use it. A man screamed and fell backwards through the shattered window, a trail of blood arcing away from him as he fell across the sill.

Hollinger chanced a quick look outside, and what he saw cheered him for the first time in days. 'We got some help out there,' he said. 'At least three or four riders just came charging in. Thornton's men are scattering.'

'It's Wade!' Cord shouted. 'It has to be Wade. He decided he didn't go along with my father after all.' She leapt up from behind the table. 'Let's give them a hand.'

'You stay here with Mooney,' Hollinger told her. When she looked as if she was about to argue he added, 'Sam's wounded. He needs you here with him, Cord.'

Cord looked at the foreman for a moment, her reluctance to stay behind was clear in the defiant tilt of her head, but she nodded her grudging agreement and settled back behind the upturned table, aiming her Winchester towards the window.

'All right. Go get them, Ben. But you be careful.'

Heaving the piled furniture away from the door,

Hollinger stepped into the hallway. Peering keenly around, allowing his vision to adjust to the gloom, he saw a shadow over by the hallway's eastern exit. The man's back was to him, but as he stepped towards him a board under the marshal's boot creaked loudly. The man swung around, bringing his gun up. Hollinger's Colt barked once and the man slumped back against the wall, then slid down it, to lie still and cold as the marshal stepped over him.

Cautiously, he made his way around the side of the house, towards the sounds of battle. Gun-flashes lit up the night like a hundred lethal winking stars. It was quite a war, but who was winning was far from clear. Garrett, and those who backed him, had dismounted and taken refuge in the nearest of the bunkhouses. They were firing through shattered windows at perhaps a half-dozen men, two of whom were firing from behind a blazing hay-wagon.

Hollinger opened fire, knocking the first man down before the second started shooting back. He was unsure of where Hollinger was exactly, in the shadows under the ranch house. The marshal had no such problem, as the man was clearly visible in the flames of the burning hay-wagon. He swayed under the impact of the two slugs that Hollinger hammered into him, taking the tailgate of the wagon down with him as he fell. He was screaming as the burning hay engulfed him, but not for long.

A bullet kicked up dirt at the marshal's heel and someone yelled for him to get some cover. Two riders thundered towards him and he hit the ground, trying desperately to roll clear of the oncoming hoofs. He made it by the slightest of margins, firing his last two bullets after the retreating horsemen.

Wade Garrett came running out of the bunkhouse, aiming a few shots of his own towards the riders. 'That was Thornton and Davis,' he shouted.

The opposition was down to two men, over by the water tower. As a fusillade of sustained gunfire from Garrett's group peppered the air and dirt around them they threw their arms high, the fight going out of them like a blown candle.

'You OK, Marshal?' Garrett asked anxiously. 'Where's Missy?'

Cord called to him from the shattered window of the ranch house, 'I'm here, Wade!' Sam Mooney was at her side, leaning on the hunting rifle that Cord had left by the window.

Garrett threw his arms wide in greeting. 'Wade's Irregulars at your service,' he hollered back. 'Is anybody hurt?'

Hollinger was about to tell him about Mooney's leg, but the former ranch foreman was doing some-

144

thing that gave him pause. He watched, baffled, as Mooney raised the hunting rifle and crouched down by the window, taking careful aim at something.

Following his line of sight the marshal saw the two fleeing riders topping the rise between the iron gates. For a moment they were silhouetted against the sky, bathed in the cold light of the full moon. It was only for a moment, but that was all Mooney needed. The Remington-Rider barked out its lethal load. Beneath the sideways leaning capital T one of the riders toppled from his saddle. The other one spurred his horse on even faster, and was soon out of sight on the other side of the rise.

'Which one was it?' Garrett called.

Mooney shrugged. 'Couldn't tell. I'm hoping for Thornton, but they was too far away.' He slumped down beneath the window, dropping the rifle and groaning at the pain his action had provoked. 'I was lucky to get one of them.'

'That wasn't luck, that was good shooting,' Hollinger told him, reloading his Colt as he walked over to the house.

'Good shooting be damned. It was that cracker-jack rifle. Where'd you get a thing like that?'

'I'll tell you after we get you into town. Doc Bracken needs to see that leg.' As he stepped over the sill he was aware of Cord going the other way.

When he saw her mounting Garrett's horse he shouted, 'Cord! Where are you going?'

She didn't answer, just took off at a gallop, heading past the many bewildered-looking ranch hands who were just emerging from cover, now that the battle seemed to be over.

Realizing where she was headed, Mooney said, 'Get after her, Marshal! I ain't sure he's dead!'

Startled by the thought that Cord could be riding into harm's way, Hollinger looked around for a mount. Garrett shouted to the young ranch hand Hollinger had seen coming out of the bunkhouse with him. The boy rounded up his own cow pony and handed the reins to the marshal.

'He's a mite faster than the one Miss Cordelia took off on,' he said.

Cord was already on the rise, jumping down off Garret's horse and running over to the fallen rider, before Hollinger caught up to her. He heard her say, 'It's not my father.' Then Davis rolled on to his back and flame leapt from his gun.

Hollinger pumped a full load into his chest, before spinning around to see Cord staggering backwards, beginning a slow fall. The blood that covered her shirt front looked almost black in the moonlight. Hollinger caught her in his arms before she hit the ground.

Stretched out under the iron T, she clutched at

his arm, pulling him close. Her voice, sounding weak and already far away, whispered to him. 'I'm so sorry, Ben.'

CHAPTER FOURTEEN

THE LAST KILLING

The wagon thundered away from the iron gates, the horses going flat out down the far side of the rise. Wade Garrett watched them go, his normally ruddy face looking pale in the moonlight.

Beside him, the young horse wrangler said, 'You think she's hurt bad? You think she'll make it?'

Garrett took the night air deep into his lungs. 'If it was anyone else, I'd be hard pushed to say for sure, but that's Cordelia Thornton, so yeah, I think she'll make it. Missy is as tough as they come.' He turned to look at Jacob Newby. 'We got work to do. We gotta round up Harker and any others who might side

148

with him. Davis is dead, but the man that started all this is still on the loose, so some folk might still be hankering after that bounty.'

Newby muttered to himself as he mounted his pony. 'The boss is still alive, but not for long I reckon. Not once the marshal catches up to him.'

Miles Bracken heard them first. He stepped out of the marshal's office and peered off down the deserted street. Midnight was long gone. Even the most determined of the drifters and bounty hunters were asleep. The town was mostly in darkness. Lamps were lit in only two buildings along Bradley Street: the marshal's office and the saloon. Only the drumming hoofs and rattling wheels of a fast-moving wagon broke the silence.

Jake Fallon and Frank Orchin joined him on the boardwalk.

'By God! I think it's them!' Bracken said, as the wagon came into view.

'Why are they coming in so fast?' Jake asked.

'Something's wrong!' Bracken told him, hurrying forward.

He could see a frightened looking Ben Hollinger up in the driving seat, with the Tumbling T foreman, Sam Mooney, sitting behind him in the well of the wagon. If Hollinger was frightened, then something very serious was wrong. As he ran towards the wagon,

Bracken was fearful of what he was about to find.

The marshal called out to him. 'Cord's been shot!'

The tailgate had barely been dropped before Bracken was climbing up into the wagon. He hunched over Cord, prising her bloodstained hands away from her stomach. Hollinger had opened her shirt, but hadn't been able to see much in the bloody mess. She wasn't gut-shot or she'd have been screaming in agony, that was something. But her eyes were glazed over, and a sheen of ice-cold sweat glistened on her skin. She moaned once as Bracken examined her. She was still conscious.

Hollinger watched, his jaw set, hope and fear all running together inside him. He said, 'The way it's all bent out of shape, I'd say the slug hit her belt buckle before going into her.'

Bracken looked at the buckle. 'Yes, I see. I think you're right. Frank, go get the bag from my office.' He turned to Hollinger. 'We have to get her inside. What about Mooney?' The foreman had passed out the moment Bracken climbed into the wagon.

'Leg wound.'

'OK. My patients are mounting up. Jake, lend a hand here.'

Jake came around to the back of the wagon. He said, 'Thornton rode in a half-hour ago. He's holed up in the saloon. Looks scared half to death. Saul

Quist is in there too. He wouldn't leave when Leila tried to close up, seemed to sense things were coming to a head, so she's in there with him. She's just watching him sitting there, waiting for you, like he has been since he rode in. What happened out there marshal?'

Bracken waved an impatient hand at him. 'We'll have time for that later. We have to get these two inside first.'

Frank Orchin was headed around the side of his store, taking the stairs up to Bracken's office, when the batwing doors of the Remuda saloon swung outwards.

Hollinger was too concerned with Cord to see the man who stepped off the boardwalk. It was only when a smooth, satisfied voice called out across the street that he turned to see Saul Quist strolling towards him, resplendent in his pearl-grey frock-coat even at that hour of the morning.

'I knew if I just waited long enough, you'd come to me. They always do.'

Jake Fallon looked over at him and shouted, 'It's over, Quist. There ain't no bounty no more.'

'The hell there ain't!' Nate Thornton had followed Quist out of the saloon. 'I'll double that bounty, Quist, if you take them both.'

Quist stopped a few feet away from the wagon, a wide grin stretching his lips. He stroked thoughtfully at the point of his beard, before saying, 'You got a deal, Mr Thornton.' He dropped his hands close to the red sash and the twin pistols that were lodged there. The fingers of his right hand tapped lovingly on an ivory grip. 'Now which of you two gentlemen wants to be the first to play? Perhaps you'd like to go together? If that's your wish, I'm right sure I can accommodate you.'

His confidence was chilling. Hollinger said, 'You stay where you are, Jake.'

'Quite right,' Quist said. 'You're a gentleman, sir. Let's leave the amateurs out of this for the present. Come on down, marshal. I'm eager to make your acquaintance after you've kept me waiting all this time.' He pointed a long finger towards Fallon. 'I can see a foolish thought taking form in that thick young skull. You'll be dead long before it crosses into becoming a deed. Just be patient. You'll have the next dance. I have you marked on my card.'

As Hollinger climbed down from the wagon, Fallon hissed. 'Ben! Don't do it! Not like this! You ain't got a prayer against him.'

'Your deputy is quite right,' the shootist gloated. 'But you have to try, don't you, marshal?'

As the two men faced each other, the silence seemed to deepen in anticipation of sudden death. People were drifting into the street now, townsfolk and drifters alike, summoned by the voices around the wagon. Leila Wendel stood just outside the saloon doors, her hair all messed up and her eyes tired and worried. Judge Bradley was hurrying down the street, hatless and coatless and adjusting his braces as he came. He was calling out urgently, but no one heard what he was saying. Everyone's attention was on the two men who stood in front of the wagon, facing each other with such deadly intent.

Quist's eyes were twin gun-sights. His hands were still, his pistols still resting in the red sash. In a moment they would explode into a blur of death-dealing motion.

Then a wild cry shattered the silence, followed by Leila's panicked shout, 'Sally! No! Stop her someone!'

It was too late. A red-haired fury ran at Quist, both fists battering at him with an uncontrollable frenzy. As Quist tried to throw her off, Sally raked her nails down the side of his face. Quist yelled in anger and drew back his fist, knocking her to the ground.

As she tried to scramble up again, Quist rounded on the marshal, the blood surging into his cheeks in a hot stain of rage. A furious anger overtook him, and it was his undoing. Hollinger's Colt had barely cleared leather before the shootist's guns were spewing lead in his direction. But in his rage his first two shots missed. One plucked at the sleeve of the marshal's sheepskin coat, the second went slightly

153

wide. As the ivory-handled pistols sang their song of death, Hollinger stood his ground and fired back. One shot.

Quist did a half-turn, a look of startled surprise on his face. Then his legs buckled and he went into a slow, twisting collapse. His guns went on firing, blowing holes in the dirt at his feet, raising a cloud of dust. By the time the dust was swirling around his head, his eyes were empty of life.

Bracken looked down at the body, a pistol still held in each hand. He muttered to himself. 'No sir, blind rage sure can't be useful in that line of work.'

Fallon heard him and asked what he'd said. Bracken smiled. 'He told me that when he gets angry someone gets dead. He didn't reckon he'd be the one dying.'

Fallon started to smile, then yelled in pain and shock as a bullet took him in the right shoulder, deadening his gun-arm instantly.

Nate Thornton, his own face now twisted in a mindless fury, was walking towards the wagon, shooting wildly. Slugs hammered into the driver's seat, close to where the marshal was standing, the Colt still in his hand. He swung his gun-arm up, taking aim, but as his finger began exerting its deadly pressure on the trigger, he saw Cord's horrified, bloodless face as her brother died almost at her feet.

I killed her brother, he told himself. I can't kill

her father as well. Not like this, not right in front of her.

He heard the dull thud of bullets hitting his mother as she ran to him. Her dying screams echoed in his head, and for a moment he was back there, watching the slaughter of his family.

Frank Orchin, racing back with the doctor's bag, saw the marshal standing with Colt drawn, but not yet returning fire. He saw Nate Thornton pulling back the hammer on his own firearm, taking more careful aim, about to shoot the marshal dead.

Orchin yelled out frantically, but as he did so he saw an unbelievable sight. One that he would never forget. Cordelia Thornton, unseen by the marshal, was standing up in the wagon behind him. She was shaking badly, and holding a gun taken from Sam Mooney's gunbelt.

She pulled the trigger and the gun flamed. Her father staggered under the impact of the bullet, his eyes wide in disbelief as they took in his daughter and the smoking gun in her hand. Then Jake was firing a Colt with his left hand. Thornton fell, dead before he hit the ground.

Cord dropped the gun and slumped back in the wagon. Hollinger snapped out of his trance, and he and Bracken jumped up beside her.

An hour later the doctor stepped out of his surgery to say, 'She'll be fine. That's one tough little lady. The slug hadn't gone in too far, thanks to that belt buckle. It'll take a while, but she'll be as good as new.'

As Hollinger swept past him, pausing only to shake his hand, Jake Fallon said, 'That's great news, Doc. Now I know you've been a mite busy, but I'd sure appreciate you getting this bullet out of me.' He indicated the bloody makeshift bandage on his shoulder. 'It's hurting like the devil.'

By the first snow of winter Cordelia Thornton was well enough to take the supply wagons into town. Wade Garrett and Turkey Brookmeyer rode alongside her, and while they took the shopping list into the store, the new owner and inheritor of the Tumbling T ranch went across the street.

Hollinger was alone, seated at his desk. As Cord came in, he felt a glow of pleasure that warmed him against the cold of the day.

She looked him over, and said, 'Still wearing that star? I heard Jake was taking over as marshal.'

'Next week,' Hollinger answered. 'He's over at Clearwater right now. I think he's hiding a sweetheart there.'

'Next week? Good, that's just in time for the wedding.'

Hollinger shook his head, the full weight of his misgivings clear to see in his troubled eyes. 'Cord, I think you're making a big mistake. I'm not the man—'

'Not the man I think you are?' Her smile was as warm as the one she had greeted him with the morning after the gunfight, after he'd sat by her bed all night and she'd eventually awakened. It was a smile that might once and for all melt away all the fear he felt, about what sort of a man he really was.

'I know exactly who you are,' she told him. 'You're no mad-dog killer, Ben Hollinger. You've killed evil men, but you're not like them. You have a conscience. You killed to avenge your family, to defend your life, to protect this town, to protect me. And you nearly died trying to protect me from hurt. That would have been a foolish sacrifice. My father killed my brother, not you. He killed him long before you had any part in it. He killed my mother too, I know that. She couldn't live without love, and that was something he could never give. But you can, Ben, and you will.'

He was taken aback, as always, by the determination and the certainty in her words.

'You're mine now, Ben Hollinger, and I intend to keep what's mine. Nothing's taking you away from me.'

He gave it up, and surrendered to a happiness he never thought he'd have. 'It's been a long time since I was a rancher,' he said. 'Don't know as I'll remember how it's done.'

'I'll remind you,' Cord told him. Her arms went around him and she held him close, and he knew that all the blood and death were in the past. Things to be forgotten. The last killing hadn't been his, and he was thankful for it.

Miles Bracken was watching from across the street. He turned to Leila Wendel and said, 'Do you think she'll wear a dress for the wedding?'